BRACK BOWMAN – AVENGER

Bowman served four years in jail for another man's crime before he returned home smouldering like a volcano, thirsting for the blood of the 'look-alike' whose crime had incarcerated him. He found his adored wife Lorna had taken her own life, unable to bear the taunts and insults from her fellow citizens. Wrath and grief boil over as he sets out to find the man responsible.

Along the way he hands out his own brand of punishment on the lawless element, and the tale takes a surprising turn when he finally meets up with his quarry.

Brack Bowman – Avenger

KEN McKEOWN

A Black Horse Western

ROBERT HALE · LONDON

ISBN 0 7090 4697 9

Robert Hale Limited
Clerkenwell House
Clerkenwell Green
London EC1R 0HT

Photoset in North Wales by
Derek Doyle & Associates, Mold, Clwyd.
Printed and bound in Great Britain by WBC Print Ltd,
and WBC Bookbinders Ltd, Bridgend, Glamorgan.

For my daughter Susan Miller and her husband David, and for Edmund Taunton, a real friend, who offered encouragement at all times. God Bless.

The author would like to thank Nick Berry for typing the work from a dreadful scrawl and for his ever-ready ear.

ONE

Blood spurted from the thin lad's nose, it ran in rivulets to the corners of his mouth. The barman pursed thick lips, then remarked to a stranger, 'Soft as a snake's ass, what say, eh?'

The stranger pushed his empty glass away and rose to his feet as easily as a well-oiled spring.

'Never been that close to a snake myself. But I'll take the word of an expert.'

The barman flushed, biting his tongue on the retort that sprang to his lips. There was an air of authority and whipcord strength about the lanky, bearded stranger.

Shaking his head in bewilderment, the lad dabbed at his nose with a bandanna. His eyes were fixed on the swinging batwings.

'Can't think what I said to make that feller so damned mad,' he muttered.

A sardonic grin spread over the barman's heavy features,

'He's just lettin' out some o' that beer. When he gets back you'll find out what you said, right enough!'

The stranger smiled thinly. 'Reckon that feller is just a plain disagreeable cuss. His sort don't need no reason to lash out, specially when there's a kid half their size just quietly mindin' his own business. I'll have another beer, barman.'

He tipped his low crowned Plainsman to the back of his black, curly thatch of hair and stroked his neatly pointed beard.

'Now see here son,' he said kindly. 'I know you ain't scared o' that bag of wind, but I'd be mighty obliged if you went home so's I can have a drink in peace, what –'

The batwings burst inwards under the impact of a beer-bellied roughneck lurching bar-wards.

'Gonna carry on where I left off,' he proclaimed and belched loudly. 'Gimme another beer, and make it damn quick.'

Before the barman was able to comply, the stranger spoke quietly. 'Make it as quick as you like barman, after you've served me! I ordered first.' He turned to smile at the sweating roughneck, 'You can hold on just half a minute, eh?'

His smile had been about as friendly as a cougar with toothache.

The roughneck belched again and focused bleary eyes on him. Slowly he took in the tall, lean frame, whipcord muscles, wide shoulders and capable hands. A warning bell tolled in his fuddled head.

'Ain't worth fightin' about, stranger.'

'Good, I'm glad we're agreed about that. I was

just tellin' our young friend that I aim to have a quiet drink ... a real quiet drink.'

The bleary eyes settled on the lad. 'You still here? Run home to your high-'n'-mighty daddy afore I punch your goddam head again!'

'I'm not goin' anywhere until you tell me what I said to rile you up. I don't want to make the same mistake twice; so what did I say, mister?'

A beefy arm shot out, thick fingers seized the youngster's hair and held him at arm's length.

'Nuthin! You bein' a town councillor's brat is 'nuff for me, just seein' you is plenty,' grunted the bully as he wound up his right fist to deliver a punch.

The stranger eased closer.

'I want a quiet drink. Let the boy go an' I'll forget your bad manners, beer-belly.'

Incredulity crept over the bloated features; then, beer dulling his sense of danger, the man turned and threw a round-house right.

The stranger swayed inside it with practised ease. He released a short left which sank up to the elbow in the flabby beer-belly. The right hand to the head was a mere blur to the onlookers. To the roughneck it was as if a mean stallion had kicked him on the chin. The batwings exploded outwards as the man was propelled by an invisible hand into the dusty, afternoon main street. He lay oblivious to a sniffing yellow dog and flies buzzing in the sun.

The lad grinned at the stranger. 'Gee, thank you, sir! If you're half as fast with a gun as –'

The barman cut across him triumphantly. 'He's quick with a gun all right! I know where I seen him.' He pointed a pudgy finger at the stranger. 'You were on a flyer five year ago ... Bowman, Brack Bowman ain't it?'

The stranger sighed and reached for his beer.

'Yep. Did four years on a chain-gang before they believed there's a feller looks just like me.'

He downed the beer at a gulp and rubbed the back of a big hand across his mouth. 'I'm still lookin' for the bastard. Till I find him I rid towns o' rats.'

'You come here to get rid of rats? We got a plague on 'em! Two-legged ones! But they don't live here, they come in from Yellow Snake and do just as they damn well please. Who sent for you?'

Brack Bowman held up a powerful hand. 'Yeah, I know all about your problem. Town Council sent for me, OK?'

'You're a high-dollar gunnie?' asked the barman with a slight wrinkle to his nostrils.

Brack Bowman laughed. 'High-dollar? They don't come no cheaper than me mister. I inherited more money than five fancy gals could spend ... I don't even ask for expenses. Hell, I enjoy it!'

The thin lad spat blood into his bandanna, then butted in, his eyes alight with hero worship. 'You feel you were sent from God like a sorta avenging angel, Mr Bowman?'

Brack Bowman gave a short mirthless laugh, his eyes as black as his pointed beard.

'Sent from God? Hardly, son. And I'm sure as

hell no angel, but you're right when you say I'm kind of an avenger!'

He paused at the batwings and grinned crookedly at the barman and the lad. 'Won't never be outa work. There's never a shortage o' work for rat-killers, eh?'

The barman came round to look over the batwings at the tall figure moving easily across the main street.

'Kid, just thank your lucky stars you ain't no rat!' he whispered.

TWO

Brack Bowman swung easily down Main Street and into Slade Town's only hotel. He looked up at the garish sign before entering, and for the second time that day he grinned at its extravagant claim.

'The Select Hotel. Most sumptuous accommodation in the county.'

A skinny young desk clerk handed him a key attached to a piece of wood nearly a foot long.

'You're back then, sir,' he observed sagely.

'Seems like. You take my bag up?'

The clerk grinned sickly. 'Yes and no, sir. It's in your room, but it was too darned heavy for one man! I had to get the manager to help me. You got a dead hoss in that bag, sir?'

Bowman smiled tightly. 'Spent four years totin' heavier weights than that. I got kinda used to it.'

He flipped the clerk a coin. 'Here, have a drink.'

The room was far from sumptuous, but the bed was comfortable beneath his 183 lb. of bone and muscle. He pulled his Bull Durham from his shirt pocket and carefully rolled a cigarette with one hand. Smoke spiralled to the tobacco-stained ceiling, flattened out and hung like a blue-grey fog over his head.

He stretched and yawned, weary from the long ride in the boneshaker of a stagecoach.

'Have to get me a hoss tomorrow,' he thought. 'God! I've had a few in my time … and I've stayed in better hotels.'

A picture of a dance-hall floozie stared down at him with seeming reproach. He grinned back at it. 'All right, I've stopped in worse places too,' he admitted.

His thoughts turned to his home-town and the events leading to where he was now. A bitter smile twisted his lips. Although faster than most with a gun and able to handle the toughest of men in a bar-room brawl, he had always been peaceful and minded his own business.

One grey day he was accused of bank robbery and murder, because a deputy sheriff ran down a child with his horse whilst galloping in pursuit. In vain he protested his innocence: three eye-witnesses testified that he was the man.

When the judge had sentenced him to hang he had vaulted the dock and made his escape. Six months of hide-and-seek had brought him close to the man who looked like him.

Everywhere Brack Bowman went he asked, 'Ever seen me before, or a feller like me?'

From flyers and dodgers in every town his photograph leered at him: 'WANTED FOR MURDER'.

Asking questions became a highly dangerous business. In one town his question elicited the reply, 'Yeah, I seen a man like you ... on a wanted poster!'

Reluctantly he knocked his informant to the ground and made a rapid exit.

Eventually in a town called Tarnville he found three people who swore they had seen the man. He called himself Wes Lorens and had left a month ago on a stage to Mexico.

Bowman gave himself up in the certain belief that the court would clear him. His faith was shattered when he was returned to the penitentiary with a promise to 'look into the matter'.

After four long, back breaking years he was released with a perfunctory apology. It seemed that Wes Lorens had been thrown out of Mexico, and now he was out there, somewhere ...

A new, tougher Brack Bowman returned home to his young wife, and found that humiliation and insults from the good ladies of his home-town had been too much for her. On the day before his release she had taken her own life. Heartbroken, he swore to avenge her death on the man who had caused it. Three days later he saw a harmless simpleton gunned down for a few measly dollars.

Brack Bowman meted out his own brand of justice on the spot.

In six months he had become the scourge of the lawless. In doing so he became harder, faster, and lonelier than he had ever been.

In every town within five hundred square miles he asked the same question: 'Ever see a feller like me before?'

Three times he found himself hot on the heels of his quarry. Then the trail went dead. Rather than waste his time he offered himself as a fast gun. Accepting no payment, he insisted only that each cause must be a worthy one.

'Sooner or later I'll run into Lorens ... and when I do he'll pay,' he told himself grimly.

A sliver of paint drifted from the bedroom ceiling like a snowflake.

He shook his head at the cracked mirror alongside the dance-hall floozie. 'Pretty grubby sorta snowflake!'

The hot bath wasn't bad. True, the bath's surface was crazed and rusted, but he enjoyed the water soothing the ache from his limbs. After half an hour's shut-eye he dressed carefully.

He tucked the bottoms of his blue Levis neatly around the tops of blue-grey calf boots, the toes were pointed and the soft leather was elaborately tooled. His blue and grey checked shirt was open at the throat, where a grey bandanna was knotted loosely. He slipped his broad shoulders into a sleeveless jacket, dark blue in colour and fastened with a leather thong and bear's claw.

From the depths of his bag he took a shell belt and holster. With great deliberation he buckled the belt around his slim waist and tied the bottom of the holster around his thigh with a length of rawhide. He unwound a roll of cloth to remove a pearl-handled Colt Peacemaker from which the front sight had been filed. After loading the gun, he spun the chambers twice; a grim smile stole across his face as he slipped the weapon into its home, butt forward.

'Looks like you an' me will be workin' hard again,' he breathed.

Although the smile twitched the corners of his lips where they met his beard, the black eyes held a hard, bleak light that told a story of suffering and determination.

THREE

There was an air of grave excitement as the town council awaited their visitor. Each of the seven councillors cast surreptitious glances at the door as if awaiting the Pied Piper, come to rid them of their two-legged rats.

Will Everson cleared his throat and pointed to the vacant chair at the end of the long table.

'He'll be here soon, so if there's anything to be said in private, let's get it over with now.' He knew there were misgivings among the members. It hadn't been easy to persuade them to send for Brack Bowman.

'Will, we've heard his reputation, but there's only one of him. There's nine o' them sons-of-bitches, don't see how he can tackle it, don't see it at all.' The speaker was a nervous man with a droopy moustache which he fingered constantly like a devotee might a rosary. Before Will could answer, a pudgy man with a line of sweat on his forehead joined in.

'Yeah, that's how I seen it all along, an' if he fails it'll be the worse fer us ... them vermin will eat us alive.'

Will Everson held up a hand wearily.

'We've already decided he's the man for the job, unless one of you fellers will volunteer to be Slade Town's first sheriff.' He knew, with a hundred-per-cent certainty, that there would be no takers.

'Don't all shout at once, fellers,' he grunted, as he surveyed the averted faces.

'Good-evening, councillors.'

All eyes swivelled to the door where the lanky, bearded man stood holding a letter aloft. He took Will Everson's hand, then sat down easily in the vacant chair.

'Why Slade? Why do they come here?' he asked.

Everson smiled grimly. 'They tried Newtown, but there's a Sheriff Shaw and a handful of tough citizens; in Tarville they found a marshal and three deputies, then they tried Massingham.'

There was a rumble of laughter around the table.

'The town is named after the sheriff, must be the toughest and fastest feller this side o' hell. There was twelve of 'em when they went visiting Massingham, only nine come back!'

Bowman stroked his beard thoughtfully, conscious of every eye on him.

'What puzzles me, folks, is why you don't have a sheriff of your own. Town this size can't be too damn poor.'

The only woman present volunteered the information in scathing tones.

'We're not short of money, or men … just a mite short on guts!'

Everson broke the embarrassed silence with a cough. 'Er, that's about the size of it, Bowman. No one feels up to it, especially as those rats come in every weekend, nine's an awful handful for one man.'

The nervous man squealed triumphantly as he tugged at his moustache.

'Ain't that what I was sayin' jest now? Even a high-dollar gunnie like Bowman can't hope to –'

Brack Bowman fixed him with a hard stare as he cut across him like a whiplash.

'You'd better all get this straight. I'm no professional gunnie, I'm just a man who hates the sort o' rats you're dealing with. Truth is, I'm not a poor man, and I've got a score of my own to settle … so money don't enter into it, OK?'

The nervous man cringed under those dark eyes boring into him.

'Sure. Sorry mister, no offence meant. But there's still nine to one, even if we give you a badge.'

Again, the lanky man cut across him. 'I'm not here to accept a badge, can't work with one. I'll do the job my way, or not at all. That means I'm judge and jury and executioner … is that understood, councillors?'

They ran their eyes over the lanky, almost gaunt frame, noting the low-slung Colt Peacemaker strapped down with a leather thong. He raised one eyebrow. 'Want to take a vote on it? But if you want me to handle your problem the vote of confidence had better be unanimous!'

He had the air of a man who wasted no words, and seven hands shot up at once.

Everson lit up an old briar pipe and beamed around at the assembly. 'You have our vote, Mister Bowman, and our thanks for agreeing to help us, we're mighty obliged.' He paused before going on, picking his words carefully like a barefooted man threading his way through a patch of cacti.

'I ask you to forgive our misgivings. But you see, if'n you fail, those fellers will fall on us like a pack o' wolves on a lamb. God help us then.'

Bowman's face softened a little, revealing the man beneath the hard exterior. 'I understand your feelings: your letter explained pretty fully. And now I'd like for you to fill in the details for me. By the way, I don't intend to fail. You can stake your life on it – like me!'

Slade was barely awake when Bowman stepped into the street. Storekeepers made desultory passes with well-worn brooms, and a few mongrels snapped at them as they did so. Already the sun was promising a good day for saloon-keepers.

Will Everson turned a corner and found himself looking at the lanky man's back as he hitched a handsome chestnut outside the largest store in Main Street.

'Bowman!' he called, his voice echoing loudly back at him in the near-deserted streets. His face blanched as he found himself looking down the widow-maker end of a Colt Peacemaker.

'You tired of life, Mister Everson?' Bowman snapped. 'That was a damn fool thing to do.'

Everson gulped and mopped his brow on the cuff of his neat city suit.

'You always so touchy? I only wanted a word with you.'

Bowman leathered the Peacemaker and favoured Everson with a wintry smile.

'Sorry friend, but I gotta lot of enemies.'

'I thought they'd all be dead,' Everson grunted crossly.

'Not all their kin though ... they all got kin somewhere, eh?'

Everson gulped noisily. 'Hell! I can see why you're jumpy ... a hell of a life you've chosen, Mr Bowman.'

FOUR

The sad-eyed mixed-breed horse made light of his load, Brack Bowman having distributed the weight evenly into four bags. The big chestnut had cast a shoe, so it was 10 a.m. before they hit the trail for Yellow Snake.

Bowman had no intention of riding in and picking a fight. First he would visit the town and take stock of the opposition. Might take only hours, or maybe a day or two, but the job would be done, and the world would not weep for the loss.

He pulled his low-crowned Plainsman forward to shade his eyes against blinding sun as he took in the plains ahead: greyish soil with sun-scorched grass as flat as a flapjack.

At midday he found himself on the brink of a ravine dropping 400 feet to sparkling water. The path down to the shallows was well-worn but no place for the unwary. Negotiating the steep sides with great care, he emerged on the other side to find a well-beaten trail through a sagebrush plateau.

He hobbled the horses before settling down in

the shade to eat, keeping a wary eye on a hornets'
nest suspended from an old scrub oak some thirty
yards away. As he tipped his hat further over his
eyes the sky fell in, and he felt a crushing pain in
his head before he lost consciousness. He awoke
with his hands and feet tied firmly together, his
shirt lying yards away and a sticky substance
oozing from his beard and running down on to his
chest. Cautiously he licked at it, and discovered it
was sweet.

'That's right Bowman, syrup … them hornets
up there will love it!'

The speaker was the beer-bellied roughneck
Brack had thumped in Slade.

'Me an' my pal bin waitin' fer you since
daybreak, gotta score to settle ain't we, Bowman?'

Brack Bowman ran his eye over the ragged
creature accompanying beer-belly.

He was thin as a starved crow, and not much
bigger, with the biggest bulgy eyes Bowman had
ever seen.

'You want me to fight both of you at once? I'll
have to have one hand untied if you want to make
a fight of it,' he growled, with more bravado than
he was feeling.

The little man squeaked at him. 'You ain't ever
goin' ter fight no one, 'cept p'raps them ole hornets
up there.'

Bowman tipped his head back painfully to stare
at the nest hanging over him like the sword of
Damocles. His back felt sore and scraped: they
must have dragged him over to the tree by his

feet. His head felt twice its normal size, and shooting lights flashed before his eyes when he closed them.

Bear-belly scowled down at him, thumbs like bananas stuck into the belt that encircled his vast gut. 'Know what we're gonna do? We're gonna go back 'cross that ravine, then we're gonna take shots at that there nest. You'll git plenty time to think about it and get excited – we're rotten shots.'

The little man squealed delightedly. 'Yeah, might take hours … but we'll do it in the end, mister.' He turned his bulging eyes on beer-belly,

'Come on Red, let's git to it. Ain't had such fun in years.'

Beer-belly nodded eagerly. 'Yeah, yeah! Hope you enjoy it too, Bowman. Hey! Them councillors will have to find another gunnie eh?'

'Assholes!' Bowman gritted. 'If you shoot like you fight, you'll never hit that nest in a million years!'

Beer-belly snorted and kicked him in the ribs, and the little man followed suit.

Bowman watched them toiling up the other side of the ravine, pulling and cursing at their horses in the blazing sun.

'Don't fall and break your necks, will you?' he muttered.

Beer-belly and his companion settled down just below the top of the ravine, a large flat rock making an ideal prop for their elbows as they aimed across the ravine.

'Kin hardly see it, Red,' protested the little man. 'Kin you?'

'I could, if'n the blamed sweat 'ud keep outa my eyes ... but I kin allus change my mind, eh?'

'Change your mind? How'd you mean, Red?'

'Shoot the bastard where he's lyin'. Now let's stir them hornets up; pity to waste that there syrup on Bowman.'

Shots rained like hail in and over the trees and scrub around Brack Bowman but the nest remained undisturbed. It would be a painful death, not quick either, he reflected. Let's hope one of 'em shoots me by mistake.

Beer-belly took a pull at a hip-flask, then rubbed sweat from his brow with the back of his hand. 'Right y'are pardner,' he growled. 'Ten dollars says I'll hit that damned nest afore you do.'

The bulgy eyes seemed about to fall from their sockets at this suggestion. 'Ten dollars?' he shrilled. 'I ain't got no ten dollars to go bettin' with you ... and I'm payin' fer these shells myself 'cos you said the bastard hit you, but givin' you ten dollars is plain ridiculous, so fergit it, Red.'

A gravelly voice behind them froze their blood.

'Don't move a muscle or you'll feed the crows ... and they'd get a good feed outa you, fat man! Now, what's going on here?'

'Feller punched me around a bit in town, jest 'cos I smacked a brat on his nose. Ain't no one gits away with that, mister.'

'No,' yammered the little man, 'so we're gonna

feed him to the hornets … it's great fun. Have a go mister.'

He turned his head as he spoke and the ancient rifle swung in his hand.

A single shell from a Colt Dragoon .44 went in one bulgy eye and straight through his head, blood spurting into a red pool on the rocky ledge.

Beer-belly's rifle was empty. He felt his pants going wet as fear made his belly wobble. He needed the consolation from his hip-flask … so he reached behind him. A .44 slug tore through his neck and out of his throat, and the torrent of blood mixed with the little man's on the ledge.

The owner of the big old Colt realized too late that Beer-belly had not been reaching for a pistol.

'Shit,' he drawled. 'You might say that your downfall was drink, fat man.'

He glanced across the ravine. 'That's no way for a man to die, I'd better get down there real quick.'

Brack Bowman was listening intently. What on earth was the meaning of those shots? His keen ears told him the difference between rifle fire and revolvers.

Minutes went past, and there was no more firing. Only the sound of angry hornets troubled him and made him sweat.

What in hell were those two bastards playing at? Were they just making him squirm for a bit longer? Suddenly a tall figure loomed over him, and his bonds were severed with a wicked looking knife.

Rescuer and rescued stared at each other in astonishment, each stroking a neat, pointed beard before running a hand through black curly hair.

'Them hornets look a bit mean. Let's get outa here friend,' Wes Lorens said quietly. 'We got a lot to discuss eh?'

Brack Bowman smiled tightly. 'First I gotta say thanks for saving my life. Never thought I'd ever say thanks to you Mister Lorens ... it's a funny old world, and that's for sure!'

FIVE

No doubt about it, Lorens was almost a mirror-image of Brack Bowman. Not exact, but almost: at 203 lb. he was about 30 lb. heavier, and his neatly pointed beard was peppered with grey flecks. He ran an appraising eye over Bowman.

'Took your gun did they?' he asked sympathetically.

Bowman scowled. 'Chucked it in the damn scrub; never find it now.'

Lorens strolled over to where the scrub thinned out. He grinned at Bowman as he bent to retrieve the weapon.

'You're lucky, friend. Blessed are the Peacemakers, as the Bible says!'

He emptied the shells into his hand before handing the gun back to Bowman. He smiled wryly. 'Don't want any shootin' before we've had a talk, eh?'

The hornets were buzzing angrily round the nest. There was a deep, menacing note in the air that caused the men to move hurriedly away to where their hobbled horses were whickering to each other.

'I know how you must feel about me but –'

'Know how I feel?' retorted Brack Bowman. 'You ain't no idea how I've been feelin' … so I'll tell you what you done to me, Lorens.'

Lorens sat back and listened without interrupting, occasionally nodding his head and chewing on a match. When Bowman had finished, Lorens threw the match away savagely.

'That bastard has got a lot to answer for,' he muttered under his breath.

'Who? You're the one that –'

'Snell.'

'Snell? The Mayor of Grainville? He allus seemed a decent feller to me. How does he fit into this?' Bowman demanded angrily.

'Not Phil. I'm talkin' about his cousin Carl. He owns a spread about four miles north of town. Got his eyes on all the damn land in a week's ride!'

'Go on Lorens, I'm all ears. Can't see how in hell you can blame him … but go on.'

It was Brack Bowman's turn to sit silently, nodding his head. The tale Wes Lorens told made sense and had a ring of truth. Lorens had lived with his father, mother and sister on a smallholding just three miles east of Grainville. Carl Snell had come out from England and began buying up land for many miles to the north. Then, when he ran low on money but high on ambition, he began to expand to the east by the simple expedient of intimidating and killing those landowners who stood in his way. The Lorens family put up a stout defence of their homestead, and John Lorens was shot dead outside the bank in Grainville. By this time Carl Snell had moved into the banking business and controlled the little bank in Grainville. The mayor, Phil, was embarrassed by the activities of his English cousin, but was unable to bring pressure to bear, particularly as the sheriff was in Carl Snell's pocket ...

Wes Lorens, wearing a mask as disguise, robbed the bank. During his getaway a child ran into the road and Wes tried desperately to swing his horse away. His mount skidded and reared as he sawed at the reins and his mask slipped to reveal his face to three witnesses. A deputy in hot pursuit rode the little girl down as she darted for the sidewalk. It was unfortunate for Brack Bowman that Wes Lorens had never been in Grainville before, preferring to drink in Lewis, three miles east of the homestead. Lorens explained earnestly that he had never intended to cause trouble for Brack Bowman. Indeed he had only learned of his double's existence two months ago.

'I'm sorry Bowman, really sorry. You been caused a heap o' trouble and misery through me, but I never intended it,' he finished quietly.

Bowman shook is head, lips compressed tightly.

'What happened to the money?'

'I went straight from the bank to the homestead, ma and sis needed the money. I couldn't stay around, not when my face would be on wanted posters all over, so I lit out. Snuck back a few weeks later; whole place was crawlin' with Snell's men … they'd "persuaded" my ma to move out.'

'Move out? Where'd they go?'

Lorens grinned tightly. 'Moved into Lewis, bought a little draper's store with the money, beats fightin' the land, don't it?'

For answer Brack Bowman flipped a cigarette at him, and they both smoked in silence, each lost in his own thoughts. At last Bowman spoke gruffly, 'OK, Lorens, guess our war is over –'

'Worn't no war, not as far as I was concerned, Bowman. You'd gota sort o' private feud of your own, and I can't say I blame you for hatin' my guts. I don't blame you at all.'

And so they talked, reservedly at first, eventually speaking easily as old friends might do.

Heavy thunderclouds were piling in from the west and the first flashes of lightning caused the two men to unhobble their horses hurriedly.

'Down in the ravine I spotted a cave; that's where I'm headin', Wes,' Bowman shouted. 'Comin'?'

'Waal, Brack I ain't stayin' out in this,' Lorens called.

A somewhat perilous slither and slide in a minor avalanche of dust and pebbles saw them and their horses in the safety of the cave.

The horses were rolling their eyes wildly as the lightning grew more dazzling. One bolt carved out a huge crater in the ground only ten feet away.

Blue lightning took over from forked lightning. Shortly afterwards ball lightning rolled down the ravine and the horses put their heads down and moaned in terror at the smell of ozone.

The two men smoked a dozen quirlies in the next hour, and grew to know each other quicker than they would have in a week under normal circumstances.

Brack Bowman told of his visit to Slade and the predicament of the townsfolk. His companion sat hunched up with his knees under his chin.

'Big job for one man, Brack. You ever tackled that many before?'

Bowman laughed mirthlessly. 'No. I got two advantages, though.'

'What would they be?'

'They don't know I'm comin', and I ain't got scruples about back-shootin' vermin or killing 'em any way I can. Vermin like them forfeit any rights as far as I'm concerned, Wes.'

Wes Lorens flicked his quirly out of the cave mouth into the soughing wind that ran through the ravine. He cocked his head, listening to the sudden roar of rain.

'Brack, you want some help? I was plannin' a ride into Yellow Snake anyhow.'

Brack Bowman ran his eyes over him, noting the ivory handled Colt Dragoon .44 revolver and the wicked-looking bowie knife that had sliced through his bonds.

'Why should you risk your neck? It's no concern of yours.'

Wes Lorens stood up, walked to the cave mouth and stood looking at the grey sheet of rain.

'Well, Brack,' he called over his shoulder, 'I reckon it is my concern. You chose a life fightin' vermin, and it's my fault. I caused it though I didn't know about it.'

Bowman's laugh echoed bleakly through the cave.'

'If it's your fault, there's a heap o' folk indebted to you … I've killed a few bad 'uns in the last six months!'

'Am I in? I feel I owe you, Brack.'

'You saved my life, remember? Shit, Wes! I was plumb terrified o' them hornets!'

Lorens turned and held out a hand as big and capable looking as his own.

'I owed you for all that back-breakin' in jail, maybe I've paid that off. But what you told me about your wife … I can't make that up to you, Brack, but I'll try.'

Bowman gripped his hand. 'OK, Wes. If'n we ever get outa this black hole you're welcome to cover my back in Yellow Snake. Were lookin' for Art Wolper an' his cronies.'

Two hours later they were on their way, and nine villains would never know what hit them.

SIX

In darkness on the edge of town, the two men reined up and sat on their horses smoking in silence. From the centre of town the raucous voices of saloon patrons and brassy laughter from pleasure-girls assailed their ears. Somewhere a honky-tonk piano started up playing bawdy songs.

'That feller can play. Best I've heard,' Wes Lorens murmured.

'Yeah, pity 'bout the singers though!'

The town was dark except for a few pale yellow rectangles of lamplight from windows and doorways. One enterprising hotel on the main drag had brightly glassed lamps on the front wall. Two thousand inhabitants, many of them tough ex-miners, and a gritty sheriff, lived side by side in uneasy peace. Sheriff Young kept the unruly element under tight control. His motto was 'If you want to raise hell, OK! Just do it in Slade or some place else!' The town council backed him, so his jail was seldom crowded.

'Wes, you stay here a while, I'm goin' to see the sheriff and —'

Lorens snorted, 'And get mistook for me? They got my face on a flyer for robbin' a bank in Texas, no one got hurt, though.'

In the light of his quirly Brack Bowman was smiling tightly as he tapped his back pocket.

'I got somethin' in here that says I'm not you! But if I'm not back in half an hour you'd best come lookin' for me.'

Sheriff Young looked up from his desk as the lanky stranger strode in and handed him a letter.

'Read it, sheriff, it's from the circuit judge – when he was sittin' in Grainville.'

The sheriff read the letter and handed it back with a grin.

'So you're Brack Bowman and not Wes Lorens. If Judge Kingman says so, it's good enough for me. You've done four years for Lorens for a robbery he did in Grainville.' His grin stopped suddenly. 'But how do I know you didn't do the bank in Texas? P'raps you pretended to be him, eh? It'd be kinda poetic justice.'

Bowman laughed harshly as he pocketed the letter.

'Because I got plenty of witnesses to say I was never outa this state when the bank was robbed in Texas. I ain't got a magic horse like Pegasus to fly back afterwards!'

'Pegasus? Who in hell is Pegasus?' demanded the sheriff in a puzzled voice.

'Pegasus was a horse in Greek mythology. Don't you sheriffs read nothin' except flyers?'

Sheriff Young laughed loudly. 'Well, that's one *flyer* I missed, worn't it! What you visitin' this god-forsaken hole for?'

'Just visitin', like you said.'

The sheriff noted the lanky stranger's broad shoulders, the whipcord muscles beneath his faded shirt, the low-slung Peacemaker over which a large, capable hand rested easily on a narrow hip.

'I just hope that there Peacemaker stays peaceful. Can't understand why they called 'em Peacemakers.'

Bowman laughed shortly. 'There's nuthin' more peaceful than a dead man, I always find.'

'That's what's worryin me, Bowman, I might just have to lock you up if'n you tell me you're goin' to play the fast gun in Yellow Snake.'

The hard, dark eyes narrowed. 'Did I say anythin' about my intentions, sheriff? And if you're thinkin' of arresting me now, you won't even get outa that chair, that's a promise!'

Brave man though he was, Young shook his head.

'I believe you Bowman. Pity you ain't a lawman, could do with a sheriff over at Slade.'

Bowman's smile was wintry. 'Fact is, sheriff, I've killed a lotta fellers that any lawman would'a hanged without losing any sleep. Been doin' a sort of a unpaid lawman's job.'

'Sort of avenger, eh? But where's your money come from?'

'Sheriff, you hit the nail on the head! As for

money, my folks kept the Red Star saloon in
Grainville. Pa drank hisself to death, ma died
soon after, and I inherited a fair bit just in time to
git married.' He shook his head. 'But that's
another story, sheriff, and I can't stand here
waggin' my jaws.'

Sheriff Young watched him duck his head
under the door frame.

'A powder keg, if ever I saw one,' he muttered.

SEVEN

The two bearded men entered Yellow Snake, and, separately but systematically, covered every saloon. An hour later they met up back at the same spot at the edge of town.

The two men with the uncanny resemblance talked far into the night. At last Bowman flicked his cigarette away and rose to his feet.

'I'm stoppin' at the Green Prairie, the one with the fancy lamps outside, where are you?'

'As far away from you as possible, Brack! Other end o' town at the Coach Inn.'

'We'll meet up here around three o'clock. Let's not get seen together in town, eh?' Brack Bowman suggested quietly.

'Right y'are, Brack. Anything I can do to-morrow?'

'Nope. Just keep outa sight as far as possible. Don't want you gettin' arrested do we?'

Wes Lorens chuckled. 'That reminds me, I've got a good laugh for you. Nearly got my head blowed off by a shaky-handed feller in one o' the saloons. Can't remember which one, but –'

'You ain't been causin' no trouble Wes?' Brack

Bowman cut across him urgently.

'Relax! This feller remembered the flyer outside the sheriff's office. He needed the $500 so bad that he snuck up on me and shoved a cissy little derringer up close to my ear. "I'm arrestin' you, Lorens," he said. You coulda heard a pin drop in that saloon, Brack.'

'What happened?'

'I pretended I was you! Ain't that rich? I said, "I'm gettin' weary of being took for that no-good Lorens, I done four years for him. I ain't goin' to leave my beer for no one, so send someone over to the sheriff's office where I just came from".'

'And then what?' demanded Brack with a twinkle in his eye.

'He sent a feller over to see the sheriff. He came back and said, "This here is Mr Bowman!". I let the feller with the derringer buy me a bottle of the best whiskey.'

It was Brack Bowman's turn to chuckle. 'You got it wrong, Wes! That bottle was bought for Brack Bowman, you said so yourself!'

'Hell – how about sharin' it?'

'Sounds reasonable, Wes. Don't go drinkin' my share, I'll have it tomorrow.'

'See you three o'clock right here, Brack. I'll bring your whiskey.'

'Yeah, but bring it in the bottle not inside your gut, eh? I think you're a tricky feller and might easily pull a stunt like that!' Bowman laughed.

'Hell! I might have known there was no flies on you, Brack,' was the reply as they rode their separate ways into town.

Brack Bowman shook his head reflectively as he dismounted at the Green Prairie. 'No,' he thought. 'He ain't a bad feller ... not a bad feller at all.'

EIGHT

Brack Bowman lowered himself on to his bed, the solid oak wardrobe pushed against the door affording him protection from any prowlers.

He recalled the nocturnal visitors he'd had four months earlier. He had called out and shot down the local terror-gun in a tiny town west of Grainville. The deceased gunman's cronies had attempted to dispose of Bowman in his room at two in the morning ... a creaking stair had betrayed them. He only fired twice: the first shell passed through the throat of one would-be assassin and between the eyes of the man behind him; the second shell entered the top of the third man's head as he fell over the dead men. 'Three for the price o' two,' he reflected grimly. 'Which gives me an idea. I might take care of nine for the price of one....'

Unable to sleep because of the ideas running riot through his mind, he lay awake and thought. By 4 a.m. his plan was made and he fell into a deep, dreamless sleep for the first time in years.

Breakfast was better than he'd hoped for: steak

and eggs and plenty of good hot coffee followed by
flapjacks nearly as good as Eileen Everson's.

Mid-morning, he went to the telegraph office,
conveniently located next to the bank. Armed
with the necessary telegraph clearance, he drew
enough money from the bank to cover the
purchases which he contemplated.

From the bustling general store he bought a
large, strong oak chest with double locks and
brass-bound corners. He also purchased a small
tin of gold lacquer and a brush, and grinned like
Satan counting souls. At the livery stables he
asked casually, 'Can I hire a buggy tomorrow, just
for the day?'

The man rubbed pudgy hands together. 'No
problem ... no problem at all, mister. Have to ask
you for a deposit, mister.'

'Sure. Can I collect about seven tomorrow
mornin'?'

'No problem, no problem,' the man repeated.
'You want a horse to pull or have –'

'Might as well, I don't think mine'll take to
pullin' a buggy. OK, seven tomorrow. You won't
let me down, eh?'

The man's close-set eyes ran over Brack
Bowman swiftly. 'No, sir! Depend on me.'

As the tall, lean man swung easily away down
the dirt road, the livery man watched him
unhappily. He wrung his fat hands and muttered
beneath his breath, 'Sooner upset Old Nick
hisself. You look like trouble, mister.'

Bowman collected the oak chest and the gold

lacquer and returned to his hotel room.

An hour later he left again with a grimly satisfied smile on his lips. 'All I need now is thirty sticks o' dynamite. Shouldn't be hard to find in a mining town, even if they ain't minin' no more,' he mused.

He soon found a grizzled old ex-miner who was thirsty and looking for easy money.

'Thirty sticks? A man'd blow hisself clear to Mexico with that much.'

Bowman called for whiskey for the ragged, unshaven creature. 'Be at that blasted oak outside o' town at 7.30 tomorrow mornin'. Tomorrow, Saturday, 7.30, got it?'

'Yeah, I got it. And I got the dynamite. You got the money, mister? Forty dollars ain't much to you, I reckon.'

Bowman glowered at him. 'Here's twenty dollars, and another twenty tomorrow. Don't think of letting me down or I'll come lookin' for you, understand?'

The ex-miner shivered and swallowed his whiskey.

'I understand you, mister. I ain't that tired o' life.'

'One more thing: keep your mouth shut about this, not just now … for ever. I might have to come back and visit you otherwise, eh?'

'What you do with it is up to you, mister. Just so long as you don't do it near me!' retorted the man as he held out his glass hopefully.

*

They went over the plan again. Finally Wes Lorens wiped sweat from his brow with a red bandanna.

'OK, Brack. Kinda drastic, ain't it?'

Brack Bowman stared at him. 'Death is always drastic, but these vermin are goin' to kill *themselves* Wes! Sorta poetic, ain't it?'

Wes grinned. 'So poetic it's beautiful, pardner! OK, see you eight o'clock in the morning.'

NINE

Bowman dressed carefully: blue Levis, blue and white check shirt, and a black bandanna around his throat. He pulled on soft black calf boots, properly called mule-ears because of the flaps which made for easy pulling-on. He oiled and checked the action of his Peacemaker and his Winchester rifle, then he smiled at his handiwork on the oak chest. A splendid, solid piece of workmanship, now adorned with the legend 'Property of the Bank of Slade Town' in gold letters. There were two locks with two different keys for added security and he slipped them into his shirt pocket alongside his Bull Durham and matches.

The pudgy man was ready for him at the stables and pocketed Brack's deposit with alacrity.

'Half back when you return my rig today. If'n you keep it till tomorrow, you get a quarter back,' he said.

'Make sure you're here at 9.30 this mornin',' Brack Bowman replied quietly.

'Nine-thirty? Why yes, if you say so, sir.'

Bowman drove the buggy round to the hotel, loaded the chest into the back, and, after a hot cup of coffee, crammed his hat firmly on his curly head and drove the rig out of town.

The grizzled old man was waiting at the blasted oak. He was shivering in the grey early morning mist, and his chest was thin and pale through his tattered shirt.

Bowman glanced at the pile of dynamite. 'Thirty sticks?'

'Yep, they're a mite sweaty, so go careful, mister.'

Bowman handed him twenty dollars, then, noting the man's impoverished condition, he asked quietly, 'How do you live? The mines are all played out round here, they tell me.'

'Live? I ain't livin' … you're lookin' at a ghost, mister,' the man replied bitterly.

'Here, take this, old-timer, you done me a real favour deliverin' the stuff out here.'

'Nah! A deal's a deal: Forty dollars is more'n enough stranger.'

Bowman lied his head off. 'I'm a gamblin' man, it's a fever with me. Can't stay off that damn Faro and Blackjack. I'll only lose it in the next town I visit.'

He pushed the money into the thin, liver-spotted hand.

'Take it friend, and make better use of it than I do, eh?'

The old man stumbled away, pulling his little hand-cart behind him. He turned and stared at Bowman from rheumy eyes.

'Thanks, mister. Remember what I say: handle that stuff like it was your best gal.'

At eight o'clock promptly Wes Lorens slithered from his grey. 'Hi, Brack. Where's the stuff?'

'In the box, Wes.'

Lorens read the inscription aloud. ' "Property of the Bank of Slade Town". You write a fair hand, Brack.'

'Comes from goin' to school 'stead of goin' fishing,' was the chuckled reply.

The mist was giving way to pale sunlight as they pulled up two miles outside the town. To the left, the scrub gave way to a hog's-back ridge; to the right, the land sloped away sharply. At one time a river had meandered through but now the scrub was so dense that no cowboy would have attempted to extricate wandering cattle. A flock of wild turkey scuttled back into the scrub, making 'put, put, put' sounds as they fled to safety.

'That ridge'll make a good enough spot for me. I'll be off now Brack. See you later, eh?'

'Yeah, but give me a hand down with this box before you go, I don't want to blow myself to hell.'

With infinite care they lowered the box, tilting it against a rock.

'Does that look like it dropped off a stage, Wes?'

'Yep. But there ain't no fresh stage tracks, but I don't s'pose they'll think about that, be too excited, I guess!'

Bowman grinned at him. 'I'll just run this buggy back and forth here a few times. Don't forget now,

Wes, if you see any other poor bugger ridin' this trail, you hightail it down here and hide the box in the scrub, OK?'

'OK, partner, all understood,' Lorens answered as he forked his horse. 'See you later.'

Bowman drove the buggy over the ground a few times, then, satisfied, he drove back to town. By ten o'clock he had returned the buggy, collected his money and eaten breakfast. He returned to his room, lay on his bed and lit a cigarette.

He thought about Slade Town. Today the shopkeepers, saloon-keepers, red-light girls, would get paid. The wives would be able to move around the town freely, well, as free as you can move in a town with no sheriff. Perhaps someone would volunteer for the job....

His thoughts turned to Eileen Everson, a good-looking woman quite a bit younger than her husband, the kind of woman who gave a man a horny feeling without even trying ... but then, maybe she tried.

At the Lazy Dog ranch Wolper and his cronies were spilling out of the log bunkhouses and saddling their horses in a fever of impatience. Rancher John Williams watched them sardonically. 'If them nine fellers put as much energy into workin' around here –'

'Yes dear,' his wife laughed. 'And we'd only need two of them! You tell me every Saturday!'

'Mmn, well I'm firin' Wolper's crew next week, all durned nine of 'em. It's not their laziness, I just don't like or trust 'em.'

His wife put a hand on his arm. 'They frighten me,' she breathed. 'Suppose they turn nasty?'

'They already are nasty!' he quipped, but his eyes were troubled as he spoke.

TEN

Wes Lorens spurred his horse up the slope onto the hog's-back ridge. Nothing broke cover except a tree full of chattering, quarrelling jays. He clapped his hands sharply and the birds flew off in fright. He dozed, periodically scanning the trail through an old spyglass; His eye would then take in the handsome oak box down below and, after that, the trail in both directions. He knew Art Wolper and his crew of villains would not be along for some time, but took no chance of an innocent passer-by happening upon the chest. As they always did when he fingered the old spyglass, his thoughts turned to the untimely death of his father at the hands of an 'unknown assassin'. 'Unknown!' he thought savagely. 'Sent by Carl Snell. I'll have him and his murderin' hellions before I'm through.'

The nine horses were cantering, their riders calling boasts and promises to each other as they headed for Slade Town.

Wilf Townly, the heavily bearded strongman

was bellowing in his usual bellicose manner to Red Glazzard. 'Gonna give that red-head at Bronzo's a ride she won't fergit ... hump her till her pretty brown eyes fall outa her head. Then you kin have a turn, Red.'

Red Glazzard was not only a fast gun, he had a quick wit. 'Nah, Wilf, I don't fancy you one little bit! Must be that beard that puts me off'n you!!'

The bearded strongman turned his attention to Wolper.

'What you say, Art? You got drinkin' or humpin' on yore mind?'

'Both!' the gunman retorted. 'But what I'm really fancyin' is that there councillor's wife ... Everson, worn't it? Think I'll make a call there ... a long call, I reckon.'

The hot-headed Tony Verrell opened his mouth to speak but Wolper yelled and reined up.

'What in hell is that?' He pointed at an oak chest leaning against a rock. 'Just don't go rushin' in like fools.' He turned to one of the lesser lights. 'You, Sid, jig up nice an' easy and see what that box is.' Not that he trusted the man: he was one of the expendable ones, it might be some sort of ambush.

'Keep yore eyes peeled, might be some kinda bushwhackers' trick. Anyone see anything?'

No one saw anything because there was nothing to see, and in any event all eyes were on the chest. Most of them had dreamed of finding a box of gold – enough to satisfy their carnal natures for the rest of their days. Now here was a box ... and Sid was calling in a voice that was hoarse with excitement.

'Got writin' on it. Says "Property of the Bank of Slade Town".'

'Is it empty?' yelped Wolper.

The man slipped from his saddle and tried to lift the chest.

'Nah, it's durned heavy. I ain't goin' to carry it to you, Art.'

Wolper rubbed his chin and made a decision. 'Come on boys, let's have a look. But keep your goddam eyes open, eh?'

They urged their mounts forward to stand in a circle round the object of their longings.

Red Glazzard was the first to speak: slowly, almost doubtfully. 'Seems funny to me, how in hell did –'

'Fell off'n the stage p'raps?' volunteered one.

'Stage don't come through afore this afternoon,' muttered Red Glazzard.

Tony Verrell put in eagerly. ''Cept when they got special deliveries. Them banks sometimes send money from bank to bank, don't they?'

Art Wolper joined in as he swung from his horse. 'Thought they wired money and –'

'Don't be a fool, Art,' snapped Verrell. 'They have to have real money for the customers!'

Wolper scowled and made a mental note to teach Verrell a lesson later. He was getting a bit too cheeky since he'd gunned down those cowpokes in Slade.

'Yep, guess you're right,' he agreed grudgingly.

'So, if that box fell off, the driver will be back, might be back any time.'

'Let's open the box right now, Art,' pleaded Verrell.

Wolper looked round the ring of expectant faces and grinned. Then he said solemnly, 'We'd best take a vote. Do we return this box to the bank when we git into town? Or do we have a look-see what's in there? Raise yore right hands all those as says take it to the bank like good little boys.'

As he spoke, he slipped his Smith and Wesson from its holster. 'Good! Unanimous vote in favour of thankin' God by acceptin' his bounteous gifts.'

'Shit!' growled Sid. 'It's got double locks and they ain't the sort you kin shoot off.'

Tony Verrell jeered raucously, 'Oh dear, oh dear, have we gotta spoil that dandy box just to get at the money, or the gold? Can't do that, can we?'

As he spoke, he leapt from his saddle and placed a six-shooter over each keyhole.

'Say when, Art!' he yelled.

Up on the ridge Wes Lorens watched the scene through his spyglass. He grinned as Art Wolper pushed Tony Verrell aside.

'Just can't wait to die, can you fellers?' he breathed. 'You oughtta remember, honesty is the best policy.'

Brack Bowman looked at the clock on the wall of the sheriff's office.

'Nearly noon. I don't know where the time flies,

do you sheriff?' he remarked artlessly as he extended a hand. 'I've enjoyed stopping in a law-abidin' town. You're doing a fine job, sheriff.'

Before the sheriff could reply, an ear-shattering roar shook the town and a huge pall of smoke blotted out the sun.

Brack Bowman smiled lazily. 'Glad I was here, wouldn't want to be where that was. Reckon someone's started minin' again?'

The sheriff gawped at the pall of smoke incredulously. 'If they started they're finishin' at the same time....'

Wes Lorens stared at the scene before him. Dust was sifting slowly over a huge crater which had been carved into the ground.

'Not a livin' soul, not a piece of a livin' soul, not even a sign of a horse ... gone, all gone.'

A thought struck him and he grinned as he lit a cigarette.

'Tough luck on the undertaker and the grave diggers. Yep, a rotten shame!!'

ELEVEN

When Brack Bowman reined to a halt he found Lorens sitting on his grey, silently contemplating the scene. A huge, ragged crater traversed the trail and carried on into the scrub. Of men and horses there was not a particle left. A thick layer of dust had settled on everything in view. Bowman's eyes roved over the area until they lit on an old oak some way off. There, wedged in the topmost branch was a big, heavy Denver saddle. 'Sixty dollars well spent,' he breathed. 'Nine hellions gone to hell. Sure is a shame 'bout the horses, though.'

He turned his attention to the man who looked so much like himself.

'Wes, reckon you don't owe me anythin' now. I sure appreciated the help. Where are you heading now? What'll you do?'

Lorens squinted against the sun. 'I'll sneak into Lewis to see ma and sis, then I got some vermin o' my own to take care of.'

Bowman grinned at him. 'One rat is much like another, I guess. If you can wait a day or two

while I visit Slade Town with the glad tidin's, I'd
sure be happy to ride with you ... if'n you can stand
my company, that is.'

Lorens stared at him in amazement. 'Stand your
company, Brack? I sure can, but why in tarnation
should you get into my fight? You don't owe me
anything ... you know what the Bible says!'

'Aw shit, Wes. You're just dyin' to quote the good
book. Go on, tell me.'

'Proverbs 26: 17 – "Meddlin' with strife that ain't
your own is like taking a dog by the ears". Or
somethin' like that,' he added.

'Wes, if I didn't know better, I'd say you just
made that up. And where did you get to read the
good book well enough to quote?'

Lorens blushed. 'My mother used to teach
Sunday school, I took a lotta whoppin' before I
learned all them proverbs.'

'Me too,' said Bowman with a covert look in his
dark eyes. 'My mom may of kept a saloon but she
sure loved the Lord!'

'Oh yeah? Go on smart-ass, give me a quote,'
Lorens taunted.

Like a shot Bowman answered, 'One your
mammy must have had in mind when she whopped
you, Wes. Proverbs 26: 3 "A whip for the horse, a
bridle for the ass ... and a rod for the fool's back".'

Lorens grinned wryly. 'Founts o' useless
information, that's us, pardner! OK, I accept your
offer to 'company me, but first you're goin' to Slade,
eh?'

'Yep, see you here in two days, Wes. Then we'll

call on them rattlers on your ranch. Just one thing, Wes.'

'Yeah?'

'Remember, you're pretendin' to be me ... so behave yourself eh?'

On the way to Slade, Bowman stopped long enough to bury Beer-belly and his side-kick. The crows and hyenas had made his task easy. Of their horses there was no sign.

After once more leaving his tackle at the Select Hotel, he shoved through the batwings and up to the bar. Late-night drinking was well under way but the atmosphere was strangely tense.

'Beer,' he growled.

The barman gawped at him and ran a furred tongue over thick lips. 'Howdee, Mister, er, Bowman. Did you meet up with them varmints? We ain't seen 'em in town.'

Silence, like the moment before an electrical storm, fell over the saloon.

An idea struck him like a clap of thunder. They thought he was dead! These men were keyed up waiting to make a fight of it if Wolper and crew had come to town. Guts at last!

'They ain't comin'. Now can I have my beer?'

The man complied with alacrity.

'You mean today? Or ain't they comin' never?'

Bowman drank deeply and licked the froth from his lips before answering. In the silence, he could hear his own gulping as the reviving liquid went down his throat.

'They had a sorta accident with a box o' dynamite,' he drawled.

'All nine of 'em?' enquired a man with shoulders like a barn door.

Bowman turned around and smiled darkly at him. 'All nine of 'em. But if you see an old Denver saddle up in a tree outside Yellow Snake, you'll be seein' all that's left of the Wolper crew.' He pushed back his hat and grinned lazily. 'They just shouldn't have stolen that dynamite, eh?'

Pandemonium broke out and spread through the town. Men, whooping and cheering, spilled out of every saloon and on to the streets.

'You fellers all prepared for a fight, were you?' Bowman asked the few who remained to finish their drinks.

The barman nodded vigorously. 'There was men on every roof in Main Street, behind every bar. We thought them varmints would ride in an' try to eat us alive.'

'Well done. Who thought that up?'

The man blushed, highlighting grey-blue eyes. 'That fine-lookin' woman who married Will Everson ... give us a real old tongue-lashin' last evening.'

Bowman grinned sardonically. 'A woman's tongue is a weapon that don't need no sharpening, and it ain't in no danger of goin' rusty!'

TWELVE

Bowman remained in his room next morning, not wanting a handshake every two minutes. He thought of gold and Slade bank, and he clapped his hands together as he spoke aloud.

'BOOM! Well fellers, there was sure a boom in gold, eh?'

He took a hot tub, he ate, checked his gear endlessly, and studied a map showing the trail to Lewis. Finally he threw himself on his bed and had a draw at his hip-flask. In response to a gentle knock he walked to one side of the door.

'Who is it?'

'It's me, Mr Bowman. Kin I come in to say thanks fer saving my hide? I brought you a bottle o' the best whiskey.'

Brack laughed aloud as he opened the door. 'Now who's the angel, son? I just swallowed my last drop. Come on in.'

The lad seated himself on a stool while Brack poured a finger of whiskey into two glasses.

'Thanks for this son, but there was no need. Just be more careful of the sort o' jaspers you drink with. Ain't you a bit young to drink in saloons? What's your father think?'

The lad sipped his drink thoughtfully and crossed and uncrossed his thin legs uncertainly. 'My daddy thinks it's good fer a boy, and I ain't so young as I look, I'm sixteen next month. Fact is I'm aimin' to join a outfit next year, cowpunchin' … a great life fer a man eh? What do you think Mr Bowman?'

Brack regarded him steadily for a few minutes before replying. 'You asked, so I'll tell you son. If'n you are a rannie, life ain't so bad, especially if you got a good rancher who appreciates you. But out on that trail, drovin' is worse than serving time in the county pen!'

'Go on! Don't seem possible, with due respect, sir.'

'Them cattle barons don't like paying if'n they can avoid it. All them young kids sign contracts – fer their own protection their folk think – but it's a way of not paying 'em: they sack the kids after a drive. Believe this son: no smoking; no swearin'; no drink; no women. The food you get is worse than hog-swill, and there ain't much of it. You kin bake to death all day on a sixty-mile ride; at night yore balls get froze off. Most cowboys die by being dragged to death when they fall from the saddle exhausted; most of 'em that are left get killed by lightnin'. Come the winter they get laid off, and use up their tiny bit of pay before the next drive. In a word son, forget it!'

A wiser lad left the hotel, and Brack Bowman

dozed with a smile on his lips. Someone had to tell him the truth!

Most of the ride to Lewis was along the floor of a narrow, forbidding ravine, silencing conversation with a crushing feeling of impending disaster. As they left the dark slash in the land behind them, their spirits lifted rapidly.

'Sure glad to be outta there,' Wes observed. 'Spooky as a graveyard at midnight.'

Brack chuckled. 'Been robbin' graves, have you, Wes?'

Brack Bowman's load of bitterness lifted from him as the light-hearted banter went on. The terrain became flat and dry, the scrub was weak and parched and even the glowing tips on the Wolf's Candle bowed over as if contemplating their roots. Three miles ouside Lewis they stopped and made a meal of jerky and java beans. Wes Lorens pointed out a low line of hills lying to the west. The plan was for Brack to camp in the hills whilst Wes sneaked into town under cover of darkness to visit his family.

Brack handed him a carefully folded letter. 'Better take this, Wes. If you get arrested you can say you're me, lookin' to see if that rat Lorens is in town!'

'A mighty valuable piece of paper, Brack. Suppose I just took off with it?' Wes teased.

Brack's eyes became hard, black marbles for a moment. 'Then you'd have to keep lookin' over

your shoulder, pardner. I'd track you clear to hell
if I had to.'

Wes grinned. 'Relax. I'd sooner run from a posse
and the whole Sioux tribe!'

As darkness fell, Brack rolled into his tarp and
gazed thoughtfully towards the embers of his
campfire. Somewhere far off a coyote was splitting
the air with screams like a soul in torment. A
bullbat swooped low enough for him to reach out
and grab if he had a mind to. A faint rumble off in
the west caused him to roll over and lean on an
elbow, listening intently. The second rumble was
louder and nearer. With the unnatural silence
that ensued, the air became thicker and warmer.

'Shit! I can't swim,' he growled to himself.

But it didn't rain.

A prolonged sigh of wind made his hobbled
horse nicker fearfully.

The first flash of lightning flared, lighting the
hills weirdly. Brack frowned and counted aloud
after each rumble echoed around the hills.

'One, two, three, four. Damn close.'

The air was a dense, oppressive cloak threatening to smother him. Hard on the heels of the next
brilliant flash came a pulverizing clap of thunder.
A smell of sulphur stung his nostrils and had his
horse shuffling and snorting in panic. He rolled
out of his tarp to soothe the animal with gentle
hands and soft words while chain lightning cut
the sky. The storm passed as quickly as it came,
but the sulphur lingered in Brack's nose until

daybreak, and three mugs of strong coffee failed to wash the taste from his tongue. The day passed, as like a three-legged tortoise, for Brack, became restless by late afternoon. Finally he decided to have a careful mosey around to locate the former home of the Lorens family and get the lie of the land. Wes wouldn't come back before dark, piece of paper or no piece of paper! No sense in walking into trouble. Following Lorens's directions he soon found himself on a hog's-back ridge looking down at the ranch.

A large horseshoe of tall firs shaded the big adobe ranch house and the outbuildings comprising two stone built outhouses and a long pine bunkhouse. End-on to the bunkhouse were three corrals containing horses. A swift, narrow stream sparkled across the land about two hundred yards from the ranch house, and access to the area was gained by a wide, gated bridge. The whole area of around six hundred square yards was enclosed by a neat wooden fence. Between the ranch house and the bunkhouse were a flagpole and a well.

He reached for his Bull Durham and built a quirly as he drank in the vista laid out below him. Sunk in thought, he rode back to where he had arranged to meet Wes Lorens.

'Goddam Carl Snell and every one o' them murderin' hellions,' he whispered to himself. 'That worn't the biggest ranch I ever saw, but sure was the prettiest. A man should be able to live contented, bring up his family peaceful.'

His Colt Peacemaker seemed to leap into his

hand, its cold, blue-black barrel glinting in the
setting sun. He checked its action carefully, then,
almost regretfully, leathered it on his thigh.

'We'll get that land back for ole Wes, sure as my
name's Bowman,' he breathed fiercely.

He dismounted stiffly. A lot of miles in a few
days could make the fittest man creak and groan
but a mug of hot coffee with a dash of rye-whiskey
had him humming under his breath.

'Don't move a muscle, mister, just turn round
nice an' slow so's I can git a good look at you,' a
voice grated close behind him.

'You'll be disappointed, friend, I ain't very
pretty,' Bowman drawled as he turned to face the
voice.

'I bin watchin' you. Yep, You're Wes Lorens all
right. That'll be another $500 fer me.'

'Aw shit! Not again. Listen, my friend, my
name's Bowman.' And he told the man as much as
he needed to know without saying anything about
his meeting with Wes. 'So you see, friend, I had
the same idea as you, I thought Lorens might be
hangin' around these parts,' Bowman concluded.

The man had listened intently to Brack
Bowman's tale and now he sat silently, wrapped
in thought. Bowman took in the stranger's
appearance and did some thinking of his own. A
burly man of less than average height, with a
mess of lank, grey hair hanging onto the collar of a
dirty shirt. His face was so lop-sided that his left
eye was the size of a bullet hole while the right

was unnaturally large and red-rimmed like a maddened bull's.

'Followed you from that Lorens ranch. What were you doin' settin' there?' he asked in that abrasive voice that went so well with his looks.

'Sizing it up. A man would be a fool to just ride in and ask if Wes Lorens was around, eh?' Brack answered, wondering if he could make a grab for the bounty hunter's huge old Colt Dragoon.

'You must figger I'm a fool, Lorens. You was just settin' there lookin' to see if'n it was safe to ride in.

'Rubbish!' Brack broke in. 'Why would I have ridden my hoss over here? You think I enjoy sleepin' out? I tell you my name is Bowman. I gotta letter of proof from the circuit –'

He stopped as he remembered where the letter was. 'Oh, I just remembered, I lost it,' he added lamely.

The bounty hunter treated him to a travesty of a smile, lips curling back like a spooked stallion. 'Haw, haw, haw! You lost it! You think I rode all the way from Texas to be took in by some cock-an'-bull story like that, Lorens?'

Brack eyed the old Dragoon. No chance.

'Long way to ride for $500. Ain't they got no one to chase in Texas. No crime there nowadays?'

The other scratched a bristly chin. 'Truth is, I'm jest passin' through, Lorens. But I jest like to pick up some easy money along the way. I ain't got to take you back, jest gotta show your hide to any sheriff, collect the bounty where I like. Wonderful thing that there telegraph, ain't it, Lorens? Better be a good boy: the flyer says "dead or alive".'

The letter sitting in Wes Lorens's pocket would have saved Brack a heap of trouble. But there it was: he'd loaned it for Wes's protection, and the irony of it made him smile tautly.

'OK, I'll behave myself. I'll just look forward to seein' your face when the sheriff gives you the boot outta his office. You won't get no bounty for me,' Brack drawled.

'Oh yeah, I will. I kin say I trailed you all the way from Texas. To save trouble, I might even take you in dead!' A crooked grin spread slowly over the stubbled features. 'Come to think of it, that's one hell of an idea!'

Thoughts pin-wheeled through Brack's mind. 'Sure had better be careful,' he told himself. 'This feller's itchin' to use that cannon o' his!'

The bounty hunter seemed to read his thoughts. He chuckled like water gurgling down a basin. 'You kin rustle up some grub, Lorens. I'm 'bout starvin'. Cook it nice: might be the last meal you'll ever git!'

Brack made the cooking and the eating take a long time. 'No sense rushin' off to Lewis, an' this *hombre* is sure lookin' to plug me, might do it any time,' was the thought that burned in his brain.

In this conjecture he was quite right: the bounty hunter was debating with himself whether he should kill his victim here or ride over to the ranch and do it there. Might make it more believable. Could this man really be the spit image of Lorens? No matter, either way, a dead man wouldn't be able to convince a sheriff. But maybe fifty dollars would convince the sheriff.

'OK, Lorens, let's git saddled up an' mosey over to that there ranch. I'd like to git another look at it.'

'In the dark? Seems unlikely we'll see anythin'.'

The ugly chuckle gusted from the bounty hunter again. 'Haw, haw! You won't see nuthin' if'n you keep talkin', Lorens!'

In the flickering firelight he assessed the lanky, bearded man opposite him. Those whipcord muscles and capable hands spoke of immense strength: the hard, dark eyes drilling into him gave him the shivers.

'Lorens,' he grunted as he thumbed back the hammer on his gun, 'I reckon you might give me trouble afore we git to Lewis, so this is where you git to see your Maker.'

A roar punched a hole through the night, and the bounty hunter's body jerked back and lay kicking as a third eye seemed to open above his nose. His kicking dwindled into spasmodic twitches and then ceased abruptly as death claimed him.

Wes Lorens stood looking down at Brack Bowman with an apologetic grin. 'Sorry, I cut that a bit fine there, pardner!'

Brack shook his curly head, then pulled at his neatly pointed beard. It was some time before he spoke. 'I was tryin' to think of a proverb to cover that. Can't think of a damn thing, 'cept perhaps 'Better late than never",' he murmured.

Then he pointed at the dead bounty hunter. 'Thanks, Wes. If you hadn't come when you did, that there would have been me!'

'Yeah, reckon so, Brack, but you just gotta stop relyin' on me to save your hide!' was the laughing reply.

THIRTEEN

They buried the bounty hunter and pointed his horse back along the trail.

Wes was in good spirits as he told Brack that his mother looked fitter than he'd ever seen her and that his sister Tracy had, at eighteen, grown into a beautiful woman. Even though the town was small, they had branched out into clothes and footwear which were railroaded in from the east. Customers came from all over to admire and purchase the latest fashions and Tracy Lorens had hit a winner by stocking books and fashion magazines. All considered, they had made a good move and were far happier than they would have been trying to keep a ranch going.

But not Wes: he wanted to breed horses, and he told Brack of his determination to oust Carl Snell from his land, although the black threat of imprisonment hung over him. As they forked their horses towards Lewis Brack looked thoughtful.

'I sure love coffee, Wes, and a smoke,' he said at length. 'Won't have neither till we get them rattlers off'n your land, and that's a promise.'

Wes laughed shortly. 'Then we'd better waste no time, pardner! But first I gotta introduce you to ma an' sis. We can lie low there for a coupla days an' make plans. What do you think?'

'Yep. No sense runnin' into the sheriff, Wes.'

Wes Lorens slapped his horse's neck affectionately as he replied, 'Ain't no sheriff in the town, they use that crooked one from Grainville. But we don't want no one ridin' over there to fetch him, that $500 is as attractive as a floozie's rear end to some fellers.'

Just half a mile from town they reined up in a wooded *arroyo*. A large, shaggy juniper thicket seemed the ideal place to long-tether their horses, particularly as a small stream gurgled not ten feet away.

Brack lifted the bags from their pack-horse and removed his Winchester. Wes only had one bag and an old .60 Hawken.

'Hate leavin' them saddles, Brack, but I ain't totin' that lot!'

He flipped a cigarette at Brack and it was flipped straight back at him.

'I ain't smokin', Wes.'

Wes shrugged. 'I reckon you could get a mite tetchy, pardner!'

Brack nodded. 'Good, I think it's the right time to get tetchy, helps to get the job done quicker, eh?'

They hefted their heavy bags as easily as if they were mere lightweight Texas saddles.

Wes cleared his throat before speaking. 'Er, Brack you may find sis awful fascinated by you. Fact is, she sorta hero-worships me, an she sure as hell can't marry *me!* But since we're –'

Brack butted in with a laugh. 'Who in hell could hero-worship an ugly mutt like you, Wes?'

'That don't come well from you, pardner. You look just like me, remember?' Wes shot back.

Brack's voice was gritted as he answered, 'How can I ever forget that? I've had a whole heap o' trouble because of it, Wes.'

They trudged the rest of the way in a silence broken only by the cries of night-hawks and the occasional howl of a dog that echoed mournfully round the dark streets of Lewis.

FOURTEEN

Sheila Lorens watched her son and the man sitting next to him while they ate. 'Like two peas in a pod,' she thought, as her heart hammered in her plump bosom. She noted the covert, admiring glances Tracy was shooting the stranger from under long black lashes. So this was the man her son had inadvertently ruined. How strange the workings of fate could be....

Brack's eyes were on the painting over the fireplace. It portrayed a curly-haired man smiling with dark, devil-may-care eyes: a gaunt, angular man with broad shoulders, a neat beard, holding a cigar in a large and capable hand.

'Was that your husband, ma'am?' Brack asked quietly.

The apple-cheeked dumpling of a woman smiled at the painting and brushed grey hair back from her forehead. 'Yes, that was John. Doesn't Wes look like him?'

Wes stopped eating, a forkful of beans half way to his mouth. 'Sis takes after him too, 'cept she don't smoke cigars,' he grinned.

Brack looked at Tracy, liking what he saw. His habitual hard look softened as he spoke.

'Your sister ain't got your father's hands either, Wes!'

Tracy blushed, then gazed back across the table at him. 'And you sure look like both Daddy and Wes!'

Wes stabbed his fork at the picture as he spoke round a mouthful of beans. 'There's one way Brack is different. He's given up coffee an' smokin' till we get the old place back again. How's that for a friend, huh?'

Sheila Lorens snorted. 'If Mister Bowman's doing that, I think you should do the same, but –'

'OK, OK. You're right, ma. I've given up as of now.'

'Good, but I must tell you, Wesley, Tracy and I aren't keen on ranch life, we've got a good life here, so there's no point in you getting into a fight on our account.'

They talked on into the early hours and all the time Tracy Lorens kept her dark eyes on Brack Bowman, avidly drinking in his every word and movement. Nothing of this was lost on her mother. And Wes noted, and wondered at her disapproval of the way things were going....

Breakfast consisted of ham, eggs, home-made bread and honey. The smell of freshly brewed coffee had Wes and Brack grinning wryly as they drank tea. Wes noted the tension in his mother's

movements and the lines of her face but Tracy
was bubbling over with barely suppressed excitement as she busied herself around the kitchen.

Brack watched the tall, slim girl clad in a blue
shirt tucked into grey cotton trousers which in
turn were tucked into grey, pointed toe calf boots.
Her long, wavy, dark hair shone in the morning
sunlight and her eyes sparkled each time she
looked at him. She was making a play for him all
right, and he felt the hot flames of desire. The
hero-worship the girl felt for her brother was not
dimmed one bit, but she plainly saw a lover,
maybe a husband, in his double.

His breakfast plate cleared, Brack sat back and
stroked his beard. With a satisfied sigh he said,
'Thank you, ma'am, an' you too Tracy, that was as
fine a breakfast as I've ever had anywhere.'

The pink-cheeked woman was looking down,
her eyes fixed on a knot in the plain wooden table.
She was far away, absorbed in thoughts at which
the others couldn't even guess.

'Something wrong, mama?' Tracy asked, a
frown of concern creasing her brow.

Sheila Lorens looked up and gestured towards
the living-room. 'I have something to say to you,
all of you. Please go in the other room.'

In the front room Wes settled in a horsehair
chair, Brack sat down on a matching sofa and
Tracy plonked down alongside him with a grateful
smile at her brother. Sheila Lorens stood at the
fireplace and looked sombrely at the picture of her
husband.

Presently she turned and spoke in a low, taut voice. 'I hope you won't interrupt me. What I've got to say is painful enough for me, if I stop I might not get started again.'

'Ma! What in tarnation –'

She held up a hand, 'No, Wesley. Just listen, please.'

Wes opened his mouth, then closed it again.

His mother spoke quietly, with just the faintest hint of a quiver in her voice. 'John was a good-looking man. He was a good father, and most of the time he was a good husband. Er, fact was, he wasn't always such a good husband, leastways not when we were first married.' Her cheeks had lost some of their colour and she drank a glass of water before continuing.

'I've always looked like this,' she said making a deprecating gesture at her dumpy figure. "Cept my hair used to be blonde and I had nice hands. Well, the truth is this: John used to ride into Grainville, he enjoyed a small card game in the saloons, and the gals were pretty.'

Brack could feel the pounding of his heart and a tic throbbed at his right eye. When she paused again, a feeling of premonition made his head swim.

'John took up with a woman, I believe she was what they call a statuesque red-head ... beautiful and well-groomed, and I can't really blame him for preferring her bed to mine. The result was she ended up having twins and her husband, who was a heavy drinker, thought they were his own. He was awful short of money at the time, his saloon wasn't making enough to feed a horse. John spun him a yarn, which was true right enough, he said that we couldn't have kids of our own and asked if he could adopt 'em. The saloon-keeper let him have just one of them boys, cost John $500.'

She heaved a deep sigh and looked helplessly at her empty glass. 'That was you, Wesley,' she murmured almost inaudibly. 'The other one was Brack here. Ten years later we were blessed with you Tracy. So: you boys are brothers and, Tracy, you're their half-sister!'

FIFTEEN

The bombshell Sheila Lorens had exploded left the other three speechless. Tracy realized that her position regarding her mother and her dead father remained the same; but Wes was now only her half-brother and she had gained a half-brother in Brack … which meant that any romantic ideas in that direction must stop. Brack was thinking the same about her, he had gained a half-sister and a full brother. Wes was shell-shocked. Suddenly he was no longer related by blood to Sheila Lorens! His father had been gunned down by Carl Snell's men and his brother had never known him. His brother! In the last ten minutes he had lost a mother and gained a brother … and the girl he had always thought of as his sister was only his half-sister!

Tracy broke their daze as she rose suddenly and ran to her mother to comfort her.

Brack shook his head slowly. 'I'm sure sorry you had to go through all this, Mrs Lorens, real sorry.'

Sheila smiled at him through her tears. 'Strange isn't it? Your father and Wesley's was my husband. Yet we three aren't related!'

Wes snorted disgustedly, 'An' that makes us brothers an' orphans and, and ... illegitimate!'

He held out a hand.

Brack took it and leaned close so that the women couldn't hear. 'Hallo, brother bastard,' he whispered.

Wes turned his attention to Sheila Lorens and rose to put a powerful arm round her. 'Ma,' he began, then stopped a moment before going on. 'You're still my ma, you brung me up.'

'Thank you, Wesley, but that's another strange thing, you never knew your real mother and Brack never knew his real father, yet you are twin brothers!'

Wes groaned. 'Ma, I'm sure glad Brack's my brother, but I'm real sorry you had to tell us about pa behavin' like that. It –'

She interrupted, pushing back her grey hair as she spoke. 'I wasn't doing it for you Wesley. But Tracy seemed mighty set on Brack, and I couldn't let things progress from there, not when you all three had the same father!'

'Yeah, I reckon we all see that. Now, there's somethin' else I been meanin' to ask you, do Snell's fellers give you any trouble since they moved you out? They must know I'll be comin' after 'em some day.'

Tracy's dark eyes flashed fire as she answered for her mother. 'At first they used to call regular, sometimes in the day downstairs in the store and sometimes knocking the door at night. They always came in and looked round the rooms, in case you were here.'

'What happened? You said it was at first: why don't they come now?'

She smiled tightly. 'They still come, about once every couple of months when the fancy takes them. One is a very smart dresser and his left ear is missing, the other is short and fat and looks as if he sleeps with the horses! He must be the scruffiest man that ever walked. When the fat scruffy one calls, I get the giggles because he's polite and looks harmless enough. But the other one makes suggestions; he makes my flesh creep.'

Brack's face had taken on that hard, merciless look as he listened. Here it was again, the situation that always infuriated him: decent people trying to lead their lives in peace whilst the lawless element did their damnedest to bring them down.

He uncurled his lanky frame, moving like a well-oiled spring. 'Wes, can I have my letter back? I'd like to walk down-town. Don't want to be mistook for you, eh?'

His brother handed the letter over reluctantly. 'You think it wise to be seen?'

'Wise?' Brack gritted. 'Perhaps not, Wes. But it ain't always smart to be wise.'

Tracy laughed like a peal of bells. 'That's the daftest thing I ever heard! That's like saying "it's sometimes foolish to be stupid!" '

By now Sheila Lorens had fully recovered her composure and she heaved a sigh of relief that her secret had at last been revealed.

'Brack,' she said gravely, 'we have no resident sheriff in Lewis, but it's a fairly quiet town. Troublemakers from the ranches around here usually ride into Grainville or even Slade, the, er, saloons and brothels are bigger and better there … so I've heard.'

'So? What are you sayin', ma'am?' Brack enquired gently.

'I'd like for it to stay quiet. I wouldn't want anyone stirring up talk about Wesley. Tracy and I live a pleasant life here, except for the occasional visit from Carl Snell's men.'

'I'll be the soul of discretion, ma'am. But I just gotta have some shells. The streets are hardly aired yet, so I'll be back as soon as….' He scratched his beard and then went on: 'Oh, er, is there a barber around?'

Tracy cut in with a laugh. 'Would you believe? The doctor does the haircutting! Not much call for doctoring or barbering in a little town like this. He's in the right place, right behind the Yellow Dog! Which reminds me, it's time we opened up.'

As Brack moved towards the Yellow Dog storekeepers were busy applying brooms to their frontages and the backs of sniffing dogs. His pace was unhurried as he drank in the early morning sun which was butter-soft on the sandy streets. A neat town, the wood-fronted buildings were not yet weathered and faded by neglect as in many towns he had visited. He turned down a narrow alley beside the Yellow Dog and spied a black board at the end with the legend in gold: 'Alan

Bell, MD'. Underneath in red letters was the word, 'Barber'.

'Cuts their throats an' then patches 'em up for a fee,' he grinned to himself. 'Should go the whole hog an' do the undertakin' too!'

Alan Bell, MD was around five-foot six and about as broad. Hairy, well muscled arms stretched his short-sleeved shirt to bursting point. The grey eyes that appraised Brack were cool and penetrating.

'Kinda early, son. You must need doctorin' real bad, eh?'

Brack grinned at him. 'If I needed real bad doctorin' I'd have gone to the blacksmith! It's barbering I'm wantin'.'

The doctor laughed and brushed at his grey, smoke-stained walrus moustache. 'Very witty! You're new here, come far?' he probed.

'Far enough,' Brack replied laconically as he followed the doctor through to a small back room on which the door sign read 'Barber'. The room had linoleum on the floor and contained a basin, a mirror, a tip-up chair and a long wooden bench. On the walls were an assortment of flyers and Brack was relieved to find that neither his own, nor Wes's, face was among those displayed.

He seated himself in the chair and fingered his beard. 'We'll have this off, please, and maybe take some of the growth off my collar. I'm findin' all this hair a mite hot.'

The burly man proceeded to cut Brack's hair in silence. Then he lathered the beard and picked up a black-handled razor as sharp as a scalpel. 'Your face is familiar,' he mused. 'We met somewhere, son?'

Brack froze as icy fingers tickled his spine. 'No, I just got one o' those faces, everyone thinks they know me,' he growled. 'P'raps when you get this here face-fluff off, I'll get some peace from folks askin' the same damn fool question.'

The grey eyes hardened. 'Don't get tetchy with me, son. I'm the man with the razor at your throat, remember?'

'And I'm the feller with the Peacemaker aimed at your gut,' Brack grated through clenched teeth. 'So make it quick, eh?'

The shave completed, Brack stared at himself through narrowed eyes. 'Thanks, I don't recognize myself!'

'Don't thank me, you're payin',' replied the doctor curtly. As he took the money he looked at Brack closely, 'I know where I've seen you. Had a flyer on the wall a few years back, you're Mrs Lorens's son, Wes. You robbed the bank in Grainville and got some other poor bastard a stretch in the pen. Nice woman your ma, an' young Tracy. I treated your ma a while back. Hope you ain't goin' to give her trouble?' Before Brack could say anything he went on quietly. 'And I hear tell there's a feller lookin' to kill you … the one who did your stretch for you. No wonder you wanted that beard off! You certainly look different now!'

Brack's mind raced. He found himself saying, 'You aimin' to turn me in, doc?'

'No, son. Like I said, your ma's a nice lady, and if you're a decent man you'll ride away an' not cause her any more grief than you already have.'

The tumult still raged through Brack's mind. Should he confide in this man? He plainly thought well of Sheila and Tracy Lorens.

'Suppose I said I ain't Wes Lorens? Suppose I was the feller lookin' for him, eh?'

There was a long silence while the doctor considered the lanky man's words.

'It's on the cards, son. You could be lookin' for Wes. But I hope you're not, it would still mean grief for the Lorens family.'

Brack sighed. 'I'm not Wes, but I ain't aimin' to give him no problems. Can I tell you somethin', in confidence, doc?'

The doctor smiled wryly. 'So long as it isn't something criminal, like you robbed a bank or similar, yes.'

Brack took a deep breath. 'Well doc, Wes 'n I just discovered we're twin brothers.'

As Brack told the story the doctor's face grew more and more amazed. He poured two large whiskeys and handed one to Brack.

'Just about the strangest tale I ever heard, but I believe you, son. Stay in that chair a minute an' I'll do a little trick on you to make your face look a mite different.'

Brack grinned, relieved at the older man's acceptance of him. 'You ain't goin' to chop my nose off, are you?'

The doctor merely grunted and proceeded to

apply a bleach to Brack's sideburns. He worked silently for some time. Finally, after a few deft touches of a white lotion he stood aside.

'Handsome feller, aren't you?'

Brack stared in amazement. 'Wowee! I sure thank you, doc. My own brother won't recognize me!'

The doctor scratched his head thoughtfully. 'I'm thinkin' it's Wes who needs the disguise, not you. You ain't runnin from the law or gunnin' for Carl Snell are you?'

Brack's eyes were hard as he replied softly, 'You're right, I ain't runnin' from the law. But I'm sure as hell gunnin' for Snell. He did Wes an' Tracy a lot of harm an' his men killed our pa. When it comes right down to it, he caused all my problems. It all started with Snell.'

'Life is sure strange. If it wasn't for Snell you'd probably never have known your brother and half sister, and he's an old man now.'

Brack's face was stony. 'You're right, doc, so when I catch up with him I'll remember that an' pump only one slug into him ... but you won't get a chance to doctor him unless you can revive the dead!'

After buying two boxes of shells in the town, he set off back to the Lorens's place. Outside the little store he paused and ran a hand over his smooth chin, grinning at his reflection before going in.

Tracy was alone behind the counter and she treated him to a puzzled stare. 'Don't I know you? I've seen your –'

Her slim hand shot to her mouth as recognition dawned on her. 'My God, Brack! That's three shocks this morning! Go on up, Wes is waiting for you.' There was a strange light in her eyes and a line of tension round her pretty mouth.

He hurried up the stairs and into the living-room. There was no sign of Wes, but Sheila Lorens was sitting on the horsehair sofa with a worried frown on her homely features. Her eyes narrowed as she took in the handsome, dark-eyed, smooth shaven man with white sideburns below his short, curly hair.

'I recognize the check shirt,' she blurted. 'This must be the day for surprises.'

She indicated a door alongside the kitchen door. 'You'll find Wes in there.' Then she giggled, a high, hysterical sound that set Brack's teeth on edge. 'He'll be glad to see you, I think!'

With two swift strides he was through the door, every nerve tingling.

Wes was bending over a large box in the little storeroom his back to the door. Shelves were piled high with boxes and parcels of all shapes and sizes.

'What's been goin' on, Wes?' Brack asked as he dropped the shell boxes onto a small table.

Wes turned, the smile freezing on his face. Brack gaped at him in astonishment as he took in Wes's clean-shaven features.

'What in the hell made you do that?' he ejaculated.

'Found pa's old razor. I thought it would make a good disguise, just give me the edge a bit. What made you do it, Brack?'

Brack grinned sheepishly. 'I thought Mrs Lorens could do without two fellers lookin' like her husband, an' I thought it'd be useful to walk around Lewis and Grainville without bein' stopped every five goddam minutes.' He chuckled at a thought that struck him. 'Tracy said she'd had three surprises. What's the other one, Wes?'

Wes jerked a thumb down behind the large box, he smiled darkly as he answered. 'Mister One-ear called early lookin' for me ... and he sure as hell found me, Brack.'

Brack strode to the box and looked down at the trussed and gagged dude who glared back with hate-filled eyes.

'What we gonna do with him, Wes? This critter made the women's lives hell, an' he made suggestions to 'em. I'd cut off his –'

Wes interrupted with a chuckle. 'Yeah, I might just do that ... if'n he don't give me a few answers.'

The one-eared man shook his head violently and mouthed something through his gag.

Brack's eyes slitted dangerously. 'If you're sayin' you won't talk, mister, I'm goin' to bet you'll talk before I'm through with you. I bet $50,000 against your balls!'

Wes laughed mirthlessly. 'Why, Brack, would you really cut off his balls if'n he loses?'

Brack spoke grimly. 'He better believe it ... an' if he don't talk I'd pay the $50,000.'

The rabid eyes filled with terror when Brack added softly, 'He'd better believe it! But I'd pay-up if he wins ...'

SIXTEEN

The two brothers sat and sipped sweet tea in silence. Brack's eyes continually roved towards the door behind which the trussed and gagged gunnie lay helpless. Wes's thoughts ran along the same lines as Brack's. That man in there works for Carl Snell. Snell started the chain of events that led to John Lorens's death, the loss of the ranch, Wes robbing Snell's bank and becoming an outcast forever fleeing the law. Brack had been mistakenly jailed and as a consequence lost his wife ... and all to satisfy Snell's lust for money.

Wes took a sheet of paper from an old bureau and wrote busily for several minutes. At last he was finished.

'I know a little soddy where we can hole up with this viper for a few days. This here's a list of stuff we'll need. Can you think of anythin' else, Brack?'

His brother took the note and ran an eye over it. 'Pretty full list, Wes. Some java beans might be handy ... that's about it.'

Wes grinned ruefully. 'No coffee, no tobacco. I'm gettin' awful mean already.'

Brack glowered as he nodded toward the door. 'Me too, an' that cuss in there is sure goin' to get to know about it.'

During the day, Tracy made several trips to get the supplies. At the same time Brack slipped out of town to check all was well with the horses.

When he returned he found that the Lorens's had prepared a meal of gargantuan proportions for him and Wes.

'Can't have you starving, can we?' Sheila smiled. She nodded towards the picture of her husband. 'He loved his food. I expect that's what he married me for! John used to say I was the best cook in the country. We used to laugh because he'd never been further than Grainville.'

There was an embarrassed silence as they all considered that remark. Wes and Brack's real mother had lived in Grainville.

At last Sheila broke the silence with a wry joke. 'God knows how many brothers and half-brothers there'd have been if he'd been a trail hand, eh?'

Brack looked up from his plate and noted the hurt look in her eyes.

'I'd punch him on the jaw if he was here now, ma'am.'

Sheila Lorens laughed loudly and in that moment they saw the girl she must have been when she married John. 'That beats everything! How could you hit your daddy for fathering you? Without him you wouldn't be here at all!'

She turned her eyes on Wes and then looked towards the door. 'Wesley, I hope there's going to be no killing, I brought you up to –'

'To what? To believe an eye for an eye an' a tooth for a tooth, like it says in the good book?'

'Yes, Wesley, but not a life for a life. Thou shalt not kill is what I'm talking about.'

Wes flushed angrily. 'A bit late for that now! I killed three fellers in the last week, all of 'em was on the verge of killin' Brack. An' Brack, well he beats all ... he killed nine of 'em in just one second!'

Brack stopped eating and smiled tightly at his twin brother. 'That's right, Wes, an' not one o' those fellers was goin' to heaven. I reckon they was all booked in at the fiery pit for sure.'

In the early hours, as the first glimmer of light washed the heavens pearly grey, the three men left the house. Brack untied and removed the one-eared man's gag.

'Pick up them two bags an' keep your trap shut. We got a fair walk ahead of us. If'n you start anythin' I'll sure as hell blow your head into little pieces. I don't aim to kill you unless I have to, but if I have to, you can be sure I'll do it.'

The man looked into the cold black eyes and believed what he heard. 'OK, I'm convinced, but you won't make me tell anythin' about Snell.'

'We'll see. Now shut up,' Brack growled as he hefted his saddle.

After collecting their horses it took longer to find the soddy than Wes had expected, slowed down as they were by the one-eared man on foot. The sun was bludgeoning their heads when Wes

pointed to a juniper thicket at the foot of a low
range of hills which they were skirting.

'Behind that thicket,' he said as he used his hat
to whisk away the ever-circling flies. 'That's our
splendid hotel for a whiles.'

The splendid hotel was a soddy shack cut into the
hillside: two walls of earth and a front of logs.
Where it jutted out from the hillside the sapling
roof was covered in earth except for a narrow
smoke hole. The smell of damp and decay
wrinkled their noses as the three men sniffed the
air inside.

Brack banged hooks into a log strengthening
the earthen walls, then he tied the one-eared
man's hands and feet to the hooks. Wes gathered
sticks and branches and soon had a fire going in
an attempt to dispel the pervading dankness.

'Think I'll sit awhile in the shade, smells
sweeter,' Brack murmured. 'Then we'll have to get
things movin'. I can't stand this no smokin', no
coffee business much longer, Wes.'

Wes squatted alongside him in the juniper
thicket and passed him a hip-flask, 'Take a drop o'
whiskey against that damp, brother. Can't have
you takin' ill right now.'

Brack lay back against a rock and regarded him
through narrowed eyes. 'What's the plan, Wes?
We can't just ride in an' move Snell an' his rattlers
out. Vengeance is one thing, what we want is
justice. Can't see how we'll get that ... even if that

one-eared varmint does give us the low-down on the Snell operation.'

Wes reached over and took a swig from his flask. There was a twinkle in his eye.

'This soddy is all that's left of the shacks an' huts used by a played-out gold mine. These hills go on a ways, in fact they overlook what used to be our ranch. The ranch was built right over the end of a tunnel. In fact, that little fancy well was a shaft, ain't no water in there.'

'Well, don't keep me hangin' on, Wes.'

'There's small rocks down there, an' one big one that covers a hole. That hole is a mine shaft that leads into this hill on t'other side. This soddy smells somethin' cruel because the floor is over the end of the shaft. So, if it ain't caved in, we got a way right into the ranch! Now how about that, Brack?'

Brack's eyes glittered. 'So we can get real close to Mister goddam Snell, unless he knows about the shaft....'

'We'll just have to ask Mister One-ear, won't we, brother? Think he'll tell us?'

Brack nodded. 'He'll talk.'

When they stepped back inside they were relieved to find that the dank smell was dispersing in the crackling heat of the open fire of juniper brush and cedar wood.

Pale eyes regarded them malevolently. 'Any chance of a smoke?'

'Nope,' answered Wes as he indicated a large, flattish rock in the corner. 'Come on, Brack, roll it back.'

Two minutes later there was a rush of foul air as the rock was moved.

'Jeez,' Brack groaned. 'It's as bad as ever in here now.'

A chain was stapled into the side of the shaft and Brack took an oil lamp and lowered himself into the dark hole. It was only a short way down to the floor of the shaft which ran off in one direction. He lit the oil lamp and peered around in the flickering light. His eye fell on a pile of old wooden pit-props of various lengths. He handed two up to Wes.

'I'll be needin' these for Mister One-ear,' he called up. 'I've just had a brain-wave, Wes.'

'What are you goin' to do with these?' Wes asked curiously. 'You ain't goin to stick 'em up his ass to make him talk, are you?'

Brack tapped his nose, 'Wait 'n see, brother; just wait an' see.'

They made a meal of corned beef and crackers and swilled it down with tea.

One-ear grinned crookedly as he ate with the one hand Wes had freed. 'You cook real good, fellers, but what's wrong with coffee?'

Wes smiled coldly. 'We ain't havin' coffee or tobacco till Carl Snell is off our ranch.'

'Waal, fellers, you'll go a long time awaitin'!'

Brack pointed to the rock in the corner. 'You saw that shaft, it goes all the way under the ranch an' up into that fancy well. That'll kinda surprise your snake of a boss, won't it?'

The pale eyes regarded them with amusement.

'We – el. That's kind of a joke, ain't it?' Eliciting no response, the prisoner went on, 'Well, it all depends, don't it, fellers?'

'On what?' Brack rasped.

'Depends if he knows about it, don't it?'

Wes leaned forward and his dark eyes bored into those of the captive. 'An' does he know?'

'That'd be tellin', wouldn't it?'

Brack spoke softly, his voice loaded with infinite menace. 'It would be tellin' ... and you will tell, mister.'

The food still warm in his belly, the man sniggered, 'You can lead a hoss to water but you can't make him drink, pardners.'

'Oh yes, you can, if'n you don't give him nothin' to drink for about a week. He'll drink then, all right,' Wes grated.

'I ain't no hoss. There ain't nothin' can make me talk, you bastards can go fuck yourselves!' the man spat, venomously.

Brack got up, crossed to the prisoner and retied his free hand. 'First question, Mister One-ear, what's your name?'

The man smirked at him. 'Ain't no harm you knowin' my handle. Hell, you don't have to drag that outa me.'

'Well?'

'Jake James ... JJ they call me. That's all you'll get.'

Brack Bowman gave him a glacial smile. 'Ever read the Bible, JJ?'

The man frowned in puzzlement. 'I know a bit

about it, never read all that rubbish, why?'

'Know about crucifixion?'

'Crucifixion? You gonna crucify me, mister?'

Bowman pointed at the long and short logs. 'Ideal size, eh?'

JJ snorted derisively. 'Who are you kiddin'? Dead men tell no tales. I'll never talk!'

Brack sighed and sat down heavily on the rock. 'Looks like I'll lose my bet, don't it? But first I'll try to convince you, JJ.'

'Thanks for nothin', mister.'

Brack's eyes were like black stones and cold as an iceberg as they bored inexorably into the man.

'The pain ain't much, at first. Just a sharp prick in each wrist. Oh yeah, don't look so surprised, the nails go through the wrists ... don't want 'em pullin' out, do we? Saves nailin' your legs too.'

As the man sneered, his mouth turned up to the missing ear in a travesty of a smile. 'You really got me pissin' my pants, mister!'

Brack continued quietly, almost musingly. 'We loop a rope round your ankles and the end goes up to your head. Keeps your legs still an' your face turned up to the sky.'

He paused and shook his head slowly, a hellish grin appeared on his handsome face and he went on, slowly, 'The sun burns your face, the flies settle on your hands to gorge on the blood. Their pals can't get any, so they settle on your face, on your nose. I bet you're gonna love the way they'll feel crawlin' up, eh?'

The one-eared man sneezed violently.

'That's it, JJ, you're gettin' the idea, but I ain't got to the best bit.'

Wes interruped. 'Has he got clothes on, Brack?'

'Only his shirt. That way there won't be much left of his balls. Gnats an' bluebottles will be chewin' 'em off. The pain in the wrists will be livin' hell and he'll wish the nails would tear right through. By that time he'll be beggin' us to kill him.' He smiled broadly. 'Then, JJ, comes the best bit.'

The man's skin was a muddy white. 'Go on, damn you, I ain't goin' to spoil your fun.'

Brack shook his head sorrowfully. 'Sure wish your name was Snell, JJ. Right: here's what you been waitin' for. The buzzards and crows start to gather an' fight over who'll sit on your head, your shoulders, clingin' to your shirt front. That's why we're gonna leave your shirt on! You can feel their claws. Then the first agonizing pecks as their beaks dig in your eyes. You ain't gonna feel any more pains then, just the fire in your eyes. You can't even start to imagine it.'

The one-eared man vomited down his city suit, shaking violently as if in the clutches of a fever.

Wes said quietly, 'Guess I'll get this cross fixed up, Brack.'

Brack held up a hand and stared hard at the shivering prisoner. 'He need to fix that cross, JJ?'

Brack was still gazing stonily at the shaking wretch of a man.

The one-eared man spoke in a hoarse whisper. 'You wouldn't crucify me? Would you?'

Brack put his face close to the other's. 'Want to bet?'

The man sagged helplessly. 'Yeah, you sonofa-bitch, you would for sure.'

'There you are, JJ,' Brack chuckled darkly. 'You're tellin the truth already!' He turned to his twin brother. 'Wes, get that cross fixed up, eh? Just in case he gets difficult.'

SEVENTEEN

The one-eared villain kept darting sideways glances at the rough, wooden cross leaning drunkenly against the wall beside him. He had long since decided that these lanky, hard-bitten twins would carry out their threat if he failed to give them the information they sought. He licked his lips and nodded as they came back into the gloom of the sod shack.

'OK, fellers, guess I got no choice. I'll tell you what I can, but you gotta remember how Snell operates.'

Brack eyed him coldly. 'And how does he operate?'

'He don't believe in puttin' his eggs in one basket, he's got a lotta gunnies on that ranch, but that's only a part of it.'

'Well?' Brack rasped. 'Go on, JJ, don't stop there, them buzzards will get your eyes for sure if'n you don't start your jaws waggin' faster.'

'OK, OK. He's got a bank in Grainville, three hotels here an' there, plus a cat-house in Yellow-Snake, an' he plans to start up a newspaper 'cos he fancies hisself as a writer.'

He paused and gulped hard, glancing from one to the other, trying to judge how much he must tell.

'He's awful short of mazuma again, there's a helluva pay roll one way an' another. He's gotta big thing comin' up this month, God knows what it is.'

Wes stepped forward and with a huge hand tilted the man's head up to stare into his eyes. 'Come on, don't be shy!'

The prisoner's eyes strayed involuntarily to the wooden props ... no future in trying to buck these two.

'He's goin' to kidnap someone, don't –'

'Kidnapping!' his captors burst out as one, disbelief written large over their faces.

'Yeah. I don't know who: he wouldn't say, and it ain't healthy to ask. Only reason he told me is 'cos the others don't write too good.'

'Writing? What in hell has writing got to do with it?' Brack almost yelled.

'He got me to write the demand note, wouldn't risk his own bein' recognized, but I don't know who it's for or when it happens. Oh yeah, I do recall it said somethin' about not tellin' a soul or he'd never get his daughter back in one piece.'

It was Wes's turn to shout. 'He's goin to abduct a kid? Jesus!'

Brack was looking like the devil incarnate, eyes glittering black pits, lips compressed tightly. 'You quite sure you don't know who the kid is? Can I freshen up your memory?' he growled menacingly.

'For Chrissake man, if I knowed I'd tell you. Must be a rich man 'cos Snell was askin' $50,000. Said he'd give the feller two weeks to get the mazuma, then he'd tell him where to deliver it. His kid would be unharmed an' waitin'.' He paused and shook his head. 'Snell wouldn't honour no agreement, that kid'll be dead as cold jerky an' no mistake.'

Brack smacked the one-eared man's face hard and the man cringed in terror. He spat blood as Brack held his hand before his eyes.

'When? Who? Who's gonna do the kidnappin'; where will they take the kid? Eh? Answer me, you sonofabitch or I'll tear out your heart with my own hands!'

The man yammered in despair. A large stain appeared on his once-smart city trousers and a smell of hot urine made Brack and Wes grimace in disgust.

'Look, I said Snell don't work that way. He tries to keep everythin' to hisself, no one is supposed to know more than he has to, that way he figures he's protectin' hisself. We all talk behind his back but we gotta be careful in case someone runs to him an' tells tales.'

Wes regarded his brother thoughtfully. 'Brack, we could sure do with this in writin' if only we had something to write with.'

Brack grinned broadly. 'You ain't felt the weight of them bags of mine, have you Wes?' He stabbed a powerful finger at one of the bags in the corner. 'There's paper in there; pencils, but no secretary. Sorry!'

His brother was still looking at the one-eared man with something approaching a smile on his lips. 'This jasper looks like an educated feller, he can write it all down.'

Brack untied the captive after producing a pencil and some sheets of paper. 'Start writin',' he ordered. 'An' don't try anythin' stupid. If'n you do, I'll sure as hell put that cross to good use.'

The pale eyes were glazed with hate and fear. 'I don't fancy that one bit, mister, I ain't goin' to give you no trouble.'

He wrote in a large, sprawling hand and soon covered one sheet.

'You'll have to do better than that, JJ,' Brack murmured. 'Just try to make out you're a writer, like Snell.'

The man looked up and grinned sickly. 'Would you believe he writes stories? He sends 'em home to London. He jots down everythin' he does an' works it into his fool stories. Ain't had one published!'

Brack's eyes narrowed and he pursed his lips. 'You sayin' what I think you're sayin', JJ?'

'Sure, he's writ it all down in a notebook. That's what you need, not me!'

As he spoke, he moved quickly to swat a bluebottle settling on his arm. His face blanched as he stared down the end of Brack's Peacemaker.

'Shit, don't shoot, mister!'

Wes laughed harshly. 'Move very slow round here, Mister James. Ole Brack is a mite tetchy since he stopped smokin' and drinkin' coffee ... and you bein' rude to womenfolk ain't 'xactly endeared you to either of us.'

Brack leathered his gun. 'Just keep writin' enough to save your skin. That fly was just remindin' you how he an' his brothers will enjoy your balls if'n you don't make us real happy!'

In the silence that closed over the little shack, Wes slapped his thigh loudly. 'Just thought of somethin', JJ. How long you worked for Snell?'

'Er, five months.'

'So you worn't workin' for him when my pa was killed?'

'Nah, I'm sure glad you can't blame me for that, long time ago, wornt it.'

'Know who pulled the trigger?'

'Yeah, Frankie Dorrell, always was a back-shooter.'

'Thank you, JJ. Now start writin' again,' Wes growled.

When the one-eared man had finished writing Brack retied him securely before settling down with Wes to read the document.

At last Wes spoke. 'Mmn, nothin' really incriminatin'. It's all what he's heard, nothing you can call real evidence.'

Brack nodded. 'Yeah, I agree, guess we may have to crucify him yet.'

The captive squealed in panic. 'You bastards! I told you all I know. An' I told you Snell's got it all writ down somewheres in the ranch. What the hell more do you need? He don't do nuthin' hisself;

he pays other poor bastards like me.'

Brack rubbed his chin. 'Yeah, I been meanin' to ask you about that. What exactly was it you did?'

'Me? Run messages, like to your folks in Lewis, scare 'em a bit, collect money an' such like. And I live on the ranch, so I take my turn at guard duty.'

'Not "live"; you mean "lived" on the ranch! When we let you go, if we let you go, you'll move right outa the territory.'

'Suits me! I've about had a bellyful of this goddam county. When can I get going?'

Brack laughed mirthlessly. 'Don't be so ornery, JJ, it's downright uncivil to talk to your hosts like that! You'll be our guest till we've sewed ole Snell up tighter than a drum. So, relax an' enjoy it!'

'Brack, old lad,' Wes announced, 'I'm goin' down that hole, I want to have a look around the ranch, might bring back that notebook.'

He turned to the one-eared man and smiled darkly, 'If I ain't back in two hours you'd best say your prayers. Ole Brack here is just dyin' to feed the birds! You sure Snell don't have some little trap fixed up in that well?'

'That ain't fair, mister. I can't be sure, I told you. Snell is tight-lipped an' don't talk much, but I reckon it oughta be OK.' His chest heaved with a sigh of resignation. 'But if it'll help you get back quick, I reckon that notebook is in his library.'

Brack held the oil lamp close to the man's face and spoke quietly. 'If'n my brother don't come back, you know what to expect. An' if he takes more'n two hours gettin' back, you'll find it pretty damn painful until he does get back. So, if'n you know exactly where that notebook is, why you'll cut Wes's time an' save yourself a lotta grief!'

The prisoner gulped visibly, these men weren't fooling. 'OK, sure, I understand. Yeah, yeah, I remember seein' him put it away once. It's inside a hollowed-out book on the bottom shelf alongside of the fire.'

'What's the book called, mister?' Wes grunted as he checked his Colt Dragoon .44. 'Time might be crucial to me an' you.'

'Uh, a blue cover with gold letters.'

'Can't you do better'n that? Go on, think,' Brack urged as, with adrenalin pouring into his bloodstream, he too checked his gun.

'Er, er … King … King – er somethin' Mines….'

'*King Solomon's Mines!*' barked Wes. 'That was pa's favourite book. The bastard's ruined that too! Wait till I get my hands round his goddam throat.'

Brack stroked his clean-shaven chin thoughtfully. 'I'm wonderin' if it's safe for you down there Wes. Air ain't too good an' you might get lost if'n you ain't careful; not to mention holes in the floor an' subsidence.'

Wes shook his head. 'Can't get lost, it's just one long tunnel, I'll watch out for holes an' I won't bring the roof down by singin'! Don't worry, I'll be all right.'

JJ attempted a laugh. 'You just look out for yourself, mister. I got a lot hangin' on you!'

Brack shot back at him. 'Yeah, if'n he don't come back you're gonna get real cross!'

Wes grinned broadly. 'Brother, I'm gettin' to like you more every minute. You sure got a wicked sense o' humour.'

'Yeah, Wes, an' the hell of it is – I ain't jokin'!'

Wes donned a warm jerkin and filled a fresh oil lamp. 'Two hours, Brack; if I ain't back then, well I guess you can start bangin' in them nails.'

'Sure, Wes. You know, I almost hope you don't make it!' Brack growled as he dragged the rock aside. He held out his hand and Wes shook it warmly. 'OK, Brother, see you soon.'

As Brack replaced the rock he turned to the one-eared villain and froze his blood with an icy stare. 'If'n you know any prayers, Mister James, you'd best start sayin' 'em. You might only have two hours before the fun starts.'

EIGHTEEN

The tunnel was narrower than Wes remembered it. John Lorens and young Wes had explored it together some half-dozen times, always hoping to spot a tell-tale glint of gold in the smoky light of their oil lamps. He'd put a few inches on his height since then, and now found he had to bend over at a back-breaking angle to avoid scraping his head on the roof. At one point there had been a heavy rock-fall, and it took him ten minutes to clear a way through. The dank air caught at his throat so that he couldn't stop coughing and spitting, and he pulled his red bandanna over his nose in a vain attempt to escape the fetid smell. Sweat trickled into his eyes, yet the damp air chilled his limbs so that he shivered uncontrollably. The oil lamp guttered fitfully, threatening to leave him in total darkness at any moment. He increased his pace, risking breaking an ankle or fracturing his skull on the numerous outcrops of rock and sagging pit-props. One such prop lay at an angle against the wall and he shook his head at the thought that passed through his mind.

'Reckon ole Brack really would go ahead an' crucify that feller if I'm late gettin' back. He sure hates varmints!' It was a panting, sweaty, leg-weary man who arrived at the tunnel's end some half an hour later.

'Half an hour back again ... leaves me an hour to get into the study an' find that book,' he thought.

He had a moment of panic as he saw a rock-fall right where he remembered the large rock to be, the one that led into the well. His memory was wrong, the rock was clear of the fall and he rolled it aside easily. His size had increased a great deal since he last scrambled through the hole with John Lorens, and he had a heart-stopping moment as he had to wriggle and squeeze through the aperture into the well shaft.

Blowing out the oil lamp and placing it carefully on the ground, he began climbing up the side. The handholds were rusted and rough to the touch. In a few moments he was at the top peering cautiously through the gloom towards the ranch house. 'You'd better be right, JJ,' he breathed, 'or we're both goin' to regret it.'

Five minutes after Wes had disappeared down the shaft Brack was devouring an apple-pie that Sheila had baked. The one-eared man watched him nervously.

'You gonna give that statement to the judge?' he asked.

Brack stopped munching. 'Judge, what judge?'

'Circuit judge o' course. He's sittin' in Grainville next week. Been stoppin' in Lewis since yesterday.'

'Old man Gilmore's in Lewis? Where's he stoppin'?'

The man was trying hard to please, the shadow of the cross hung over him. 'He an' his family is in the Blue Star Hotel, little place behind The Dog. He allus stops there 'cos a friend o' his runs it, a real sourpuss feller like the judge.'

Brack grimaced at the thought. 'Yeah, he didn't seem too worried that I'd done four years for somethin' I knew nothin' about, but at least he gave me a letter to prove my innocence.'

He remembered the circuit judge well, the flinty grey eyes, the aquiline nose above a fluffy white beard. He even remembered the long fingers and veiny-backed hands as they idly dabbed a spotless linen handkerchief at the old man's lips. A hard man, a remorseless enemy of the lawless, the sort Brack had called a good judge – until he had appeared before him. His thoughts moved swiftly. Would it be worth approaching Judge Gilmore with the statement from the one-eared villain? Maybe get a pardon for Wes? Brack grabbed the paper and pencil and began writing a statement of his own. Judge Gilmore knew part of it: how Brack had been the victim of a terrible mistake. Maybe he could convince the flinty old devil that Wes was equally a victim – a victim of the evil and

ruthlessness of Carl Snell. It was worth a try:
what was there to lose?

Wes eased himself gingerly out of the well,
straining eyes and ears into the darkness. No use
killing a guard and risking the whole lot of them
come running. He recalled John Lorens's old
adage, 'discretion is the better part of valour'.
'Sometimes,' he added grimly. 'Only sometimes.'

Somewhere in the back a lamp cast a yellow
rectangle of light out into the night. Wes crawled
up to the window, every nerve tingling he eased
himself up to peer in. Snell lay on his bed, writing
in a small, thick notebook. From time to time a
grin stole over his old, but still handsome
features, he looked mighty pleased with himself.

'Go on, grin, you bastard,' Wes thought. 'That's
my damn room you're usin', but not for long or my
name ain't Wes Lorens!'

A chill knot of hate congealing around his heart,
he slipped over to the other side, and froze at the
sound of a man's boots creaking softly. An instant
later he caught sight of a guard patrolling not
twenty yards away. His heart pounded as he
removed a sharp knife from his boot top. But the
guard passed on, unaware of how close he had
been to death. Wes continued round to where he
knew the study to be, and heaved a sigh of relief to
find the window open. He was very soon inside the
study. Although he knew the ranch house like the
back of his hand, he moved cautiously. Who could
tell what new items of furniture might lie in wait

for him in the darkness? With infinite care he felt his way to the fireplace, then groped gently along the bottom shelf of the bookcase until his hand encountered a large volume. Instinctively, he knew it was *King Solomon's Mines*, a heartbeat later he was certain as he felt the hollowed-out pages. Hollow? Where in Gods name was the notebook? A feeling of utter despair was burned away by flaming anger as he realized that the notebook Snell was writing in was probably the one he sought.

'Shit,' he muttered. 'That changes things considerable.'

Wearily he came to his feet and put his elbows on the mantelshelf, lost in thought. What to do? Go in and confront Snell?

His problem was solved for him as a cultured English voice spoke from just over his shoulder.

'Good gracious me! A visitor at this hour. Interested in books too!'

Wes turned slowly to face Carl Snell, a sick sinking in the pit of his stomach.

'Not books, Snell, just one particular book.'

Snell smiled as he held aloft a large oil lamp with one hand whilst pointing a Harrington-Richardson .36 at Wes's heart.

'Ah yes, *King Solomon's Mines*. One of my favourites; yours too?'

Wes almost snarled his retort. 'It was my pa's till you paid Frankie Dorrell to shoot him in the back, you slimy bastard!'

Snell's eyes widened. 'Well, well, well! You're

Wes Lorens. Without the beard you look unlike
the posters. Good heavens, what a change.' He
placed the lamp on the table, never taking his
grey-flecked eyes from the lanky man's face. 'So
what can I do for you, Lorens? Please don't make
me shoot you. I'd much prefer to surprise the
guards by tying you to that chair.' He nodded
sideways at a big old upright chair at a desk.
'They've got slack of late, I've told the lazy devils
to pull their socks up. After I've tied you securely
I'll call them and say they must search the
grounds thoroughly. When they've sweated for an
hour or so I'll bring them in and introduce you.
Won't they be ashamed!' Then in an ice-cold voice
he added, 'Then I'll shoot the man responsible for
your gaining an entry, Lorens. Now, how did you
get in? I might let you go if you're co-operative.
How about it?'

Wes eyed the Harrington-Richardson. No
chance. 'Go jump in the river, Snell. It ain't far.'

'Ah well, have it your own way, dear boy,' Snell
murmured. His eyes fell on the book, open to show
the hollowed-out interior. 'Mmm, I spoiled a good
book, didn't I?' From his smoking-jacket pocket he
pulled the notebook. 'Were you looking for this by
any chance? Who told you –'

He broke off, eyes narrowed to murky slits, 'Ah!
JJ's not returned from seeing your people. I
suppose you leaned on him a little, hmm?'

Wes grinned darkly. 'Oh yeah, we leaned on
him all right.'

'We? Who else is in on this?' Snell demanded.

'My brother.' As an afterthought he lied. 'An' about thirty friends an' all the lawmen this side o' Texas.'

Carl Snell regarded him thoughtfully and ran a hand through his red hair. Then he smiled. 'You're a liar, Lorens, you couldn't have wormed that out of him and gathered all those friends and lawmen together in so short a time.'

Wes chuckled and lied again. 'Short time? JJ's been workin' for us three months now. You've been had, Mister Snell!' He was trying to rattle the man into making a mistake, get him off balance, anything to gain an edge, a chance to snatch that gun.

It was Snell's turn to chuckle. 'Good heavens! If all the evidence is in the notebook, I'll simply burn it now. A pity, but I carry a lot in my head. Yes, we'll burn it right now. Shut the window and close the shutters, please Lorens, I don't want my men seeing you just yet.'

Under the threat of the Harrington-Richardson Wes complied without argument. Snell tossed him a box of matches.

'Cosy, isn't it?' he murmured. 'Light the fire will you? There's a good chap.' He yawned elaborately. 'I'm expecting a lady later, it'll be nice to receive her with a good fire burning.'

Wes put a match to the fire and stood looking down at it, his hands on the mantelshelf.

'That's better, Lorens. Now we'll add the notebook as well, eh?'

Wes sank his head wearily to the mantelshelf as

Snell held out the notebook. Looking over his right shoulder, Wes reached back towards the other man. Snell's eyes never left the lanky man's hand as the notebook was passed. He didn't see the heel of Wes's heavy boot until it was too late. It caught him squarely under the chin and hurled his 196 lb. over backwards as if he were a mere rag-doll. The gun slipped from his nerveless grasp as his jaw shattered.

Wes watched the unconscious figure as he thrust the notebook into his jerkin pocket. From the wall above the fireplace he took a fancy lariat intended as decoration. He tied Snell's upper arms in such a way that it would be possible to use his lower arms within limits, then passed a loop round the man's neck. Snell regained consciousness to find himself securely tied. His broken jaw only permitted him to utter guttural sounds as he was dragged through a narrow aperture and into a foul-smelling tunnel.

'R' a' I?' he groaned. 'Wus h'nning?'

'Where are you? In a tunnel under the ranch. What's happening? I'm takin' you for a stroll to meet your ole pal JJ. Get movin'!'

At the ranch things were coming to a head. Snell's ramrod, Butch Collar, was engaged in earnest talk with Red Carstairs.

'Listen, Red,' he said hoarsely. 'I've looked in his bedroom, the study, livin-room, every damn place. He ain't nowheres to be seen. JJ still ain't showed up either.'

Red snorted derisively. 'The boss kept sayin' the security weren't good enough. Ain't no way he coulda crept outa the ranch without bein' seen. I reckon he's hidin' somewhere just to ketch us out. Maybe it's some game him an' JJ is playin' on us. I don't trust that old bastard one bit, nor JJ.'

Butch rubbed his bulbous nose anxiously. 'Yeah, could be. Where in tarnation can he be hidin', Red?'

'You know him better'n me, Butch. I reckon he's gonna let JJ in somewheres along the fence an' then give us a real chewin' out in that dude's voice of his'n.'

'What we gonna do, Red? I ain't aimin' to get fired, the mazuma's too damn good.' Butch swallowed and took command as the thought of losing his well-paid job loomed closer. 'Round up six o' the boys an' search every goddam room in the ranch, then the outhouses, includin' the bunkhouse. Meet me back here by this ole well soon's you're through.'

'What are you gonna do, Butch?'

'Me? If'n it's any business o' yours, I'm gonna get the rest o' the boys an' search every damn inch around the fence, then we'll turn over every fuckin' stone till we find him. Move, Red, move!'

In less than three minutes the spread was crawling with gunnies. Oil lamps gleamed and bobbed like giant fireflies. A very sick-at-heart Butch met up with Red at the well.

'We've combed every sonofabitching inch, Red: nuthin'. What about you?'

Red peered down the well, holding his lamp down as far as he dared lean. 'Ain't down there. We ain't missed a damn inch anywheres.'

Butch kicked the well savagely. 'That's it then. He musta got out without no one seein'. He'll flay us alive when he gits back, we'll all be outa work.'

Red wiped sweat from his eyes with a grubby bandanna, 'What's that room been all fancied up for? The one in the roof – ain't a speck o' dust anywhere.'

Butch smacked his face hard. 'Mind yore own business! The boss has got a good reason.'

'Boss?' Red spat. 'We won't have no boss by the sound of it. Looks like we'll git fired.'

'Not if'n we play our cards right,' Butch rasped. 'Gettin' out is one thing. Gettin' back in is another!'

'Meanin'?'

'The boss might be in a forgivin' mood if he caint get back in again. He's probably out there now, 'spectin' to ketch us out. Let's just make sure he don't get in without bein' challenged.'

The gunnies under Butch's command deployed themselves round the perimeter fence, determined that not even a mouse would enter unchallenged. A cold wind sprang up from the north followed by persistent drizzle. It was a long, bleak night.

NINETEEN

Brack wrote steadily, glancing from time to time at a gold pocket-watch he kept in a pigskin bag.

One-eared Jake James licked his lips nervously and tried to keep his eyes away from the wooden cross. Try as he would, they moved involuntarily between the rock, the cross and the tall, lean man writing in the corner.

'How long, mister?'

'How long what?'

'How long's he been gone?'

Brack looked up. 'You mean how long to crucifixion time, eh?'

The prisoner scowled at him. 'You know what I mean: when is he due back?'

Brack took his time studying his watch; although he smiled at length it held no cheer for the villain.

'Five minutes, JJ. That's, er, three hundred seconds. Ain't long when you put it like that, is it?' he drawled.

He rose and stretched himself. JJ flinched at the sudden crack of one of his joints.

'Well, that's finished that little job. Now where in tarnation did Wes put those nails?'

Jake James's face was dust-grey with fear as he searched the little soddy diligently.

'Durn it,' Brack pronounced at last. 'Ole Wes used the last o' them nails makin' that cross. Now how in hell we gonna manage, JJ?'

The one-eared man squealed in terror. 'Hold on, mister, he's gotta be back in a minute!'

'You better pray he is, Mister James. A few ole nails wouldn't stop me crucifyin' you. I could tie you on that there cross so tight you'd look like you was born with it on your back!'

The other man was staring at the rock as if the force of his will could lift it.

Brack followed his gaze. 'You tryin' to raise that rock by mind-power? Ain't no use 'less Wes comes through the hole, an' then all your –'

He stopped and chuckled, hiding his relief. 'There you are, JJ, you got the first bit right.'

The rock was moving, and Brack hurried to give a hand. A strange face peered up at him, the eyes blinking in the light. The man's red hair was neatly parted in the centre but his jaw was swollen and bruised blue-red. Blood trickled from the corners of his mouth and dripped from his blackened chin. From below him in the darkness Wes's voice sounded muffled.

'Hold that jasper up, Brack. I don't want him fallin' on top of me.'

As Brack pulled the man into the shack he heard a sharp gasp of recognition from Jake James.

'Gawd amighty! It's Mister Snell!'

Brack stepped back and glared at Snell. 'Maybe I've a good use for that cross after all.'

Wes scrambled from the hole and replaced the rock quickly.

'You got no idea how sweet 'n' fresh the air smells in here, brother! Smells like a whore's crotch down there.'

Brack was still looking at Snell. 'You sure hit him hard, Wes. He upset you?' he enquired innocently.

Wes grinned at him. 'To tell the truth, Brack, I kicked him. He's got a mite o' trouble talkin' right now. I've spoiled that English accent of his'n.'

Snell couldn't talk, but, as the numbness of shock wore off, his brain was racing. Thank God JJ knew nothing about the kidnapping. At this very moment a hired gunnie was seeking a chance to grab his victim. JJ couldn't have told them anything.

Brack was stroking his clean-shaven chin. 'Well, I was gonna ask him who he was aimin' to kidnap.'

Snell spat blood. So, JJ had known about the plot. But he didn't know who the victim was to be. Just as well he kept those gunnies of his in the dark. The swine couldn't be trusted with anything.

Wes broke the silence with a chuckle. 'He can't talk much, but he can sure as hell write the answers down, if'n he's a mind to, Brack. A sorta confession, if you get my drift, Brack.'

He paused and rubbed his stomach. 'But first we eat, eh, brother? My gut feels like my throat's been cut, I don't think ole Snell here will want to eat, though.'

Brack nodded. 'OK. You got the notebook?'

'Sure,' Wes grinned. 'got the book an', the, er, author.'

'Good,' Brack said briskly. 'Perhaps you could persuade him to autograph it for us, eh, Wes?'

'Why should I?' Snell mumbled. 'You can't mn, mn, make me.'

Brack laughed gratingly. 'Don't bet on it! Just ask ole JJ if'n I can make you sign that book o' your'n. I persuaded him to talk. Tell him, JJ.'

Jake James nodded vehemently. 'He'll make you do it, Mister Snell. Save yourself a lotta grief, an' sign the damn thing!'

Snell absorbed the one-eared man's dishevelled appearance, his stained trousers and shaking hands. JJ had been a hard man, one of his most reliable thugs. He took the pencil and signed the cover of the notebook, then groaned through his ruined mouth, 'You'll regret this, gennelmen.'

Wes shook a finger at him. 'Don't tempt Brack, he's got an awful lot against you, Mister Snell. If'n you want to live long enough to hang, just don't rile my brother too much.'

Brack got busy frying steaks over the fire and soon they were swilling down steak sandwiches with hot tea. At length Brack broke the silence.

'We got JJ's statement; I've written a statement too; an' we got Snell's book. Looks like I should ride into Lewis an' see the circuit judge.'

'Circuit judge? He's in Lewis?'

'Yep, accordin' to this jasper,' he said with a jerk of a thumb at the one-eared villain. 'By the way, Wes, he figured it was someone outside Lewis they was plannin' to kidnap. There ain't no one rich enough to pay that sorta mazuma round here.'

Wes nodded agreement. 'Yeah, but it don't matter, he ain't goin' to kidnap no one now.'

'Look in the notebook, Wes. Don't it say?'

'Jeez!' his brother ejaculated. 'Never gave it a thought!' He grabbed the notebook and read swiftly. His face fell. 'Shit, I shoulda given him time to write it all down, he's only got the outline plan here.'

'Wes,' said Brack patiently, 'we can allus ask him, can't we? He's sittin' right over there!'

Wes went over and handed Snell paper and pencil.

'Can't stand to translate all that mumblin' o' your'n, Snell. Write down whose kid you were goin' to snatch.'

Snell's eyes were popping from his head. He seemed to be in the grip of extreme fear. His hand shook visibly as he wrote, 'I hadn't planned who, it was months away.' Why should he tell them? It would only exacerbate the situation. At that moment his gunnie was skulking in the dark, awaiting the moment to execute the kidnap … and here were these hard-bitten men who knew all but the identity of the victim! One way or

another, he was sure he would soon be dancing on
air if he couldn't manage to get free and flee across
the border, soon.

'Oh well, no matter, Snell. You'll hang for
arrangin' our pa's murder. We got you dead to
rights,' Brack grated. 'Wes,' he added, 'I'm goin'
into Lewis first thing in the mornin'. Tie these
jaspers real tight. Wake me in three hours, we'll
take shifts. I ain't takin' no chances.'

At seven o' clock Brack hit the trail for Lewis.
Arriving well before noon, he headed straight for
the Blue Star Hotel and Judge Gilmore.

His knock at the door of the judge's study was
answered by a peremptory 'Enter'.

Judge Gilmore put aside a legal tome, clucked
his tongue and eyed his lanky visitor coldly.
'Well?'

Brack smiled easily and removed his low-
crowned Plainsman. 'Thank you for seein' me,
Judge.' He held out a folded sheet of paper. 'You
may recall this letter you gave me.'

Judge Gilmore snatched the letter and read it
swiftly. 'Yes, I remember, and as I remember it
you had a beard and you didn't have those grey
sideburns.'

'You've a good memory an' a keen eye, judge.'

The slate grey eyes hardened in the flinty face.
The old man's mouth thinned to a tight line. 'You
didn't come here to waste my time telling me
something I already know, Bowman.'

By way of reply Brack thrust his statement into

the vein-knotted hands. Lips pursed, the judge read through it, then snorted. 'A pardon for Lorens? Don't be ridiculous! Now, get out, I'm expecting a visitor.'

Before his eyes Brack appeared to swell and for the first time in his life the old man felt fear.

'Judge, you're goin' to listen to me. I'm a law-abidin' feller, an' you hate the lawless as much as me. Thanks to Snell I got four years hard from you. My wife took her life because o' the shame. Snell stole my brother's ranch an killed our pa. You'll see a whole damn catalogue of crime in a document I got here from one o' his men. Read it, or I'll shore as hell break your neck.'

With trembling hands the old judge read Jake James's statement.

'Now read this notebook o' Snell's,' Brack grated.

Again the judge read, his head shaking slowly as he turned the pages. At last he looked up. 'You know who I was expecting when you came in?'

'No, judge; couldn't have been Snell –'

'Yes, it was, but not Carl Snell – but his cousin the mayor of Grainville.'

Brack grinned wryly. 'He ain't a bad feller. Fact is, he's embarrassed about his cousin's activities. But, see here, what about my brother Wes?'

The old eyes narrowed as the long fingers formed a steeple on the desk. 'A robbery is a robbery. He'll have to be tried and –'

'Tried?' Brack hissed. 'Tried an' sentenced like I was? I'll send you to hell first!'

There was a gentle tap at the door. 'May I come in, dear?'

Judge Gilmore sighed. 'Yes Cynthia, come in.'

A good-looking woman of around fifty sidled timidly into the room.

'A man left this letter for you, and Mayor Snell is waiting to see you dear.'

'Thank you. Well, what are you waiting for?' the judge demanded.

She spoke hesitantly. 'Um, er, Rachel –'

'Rachel?' The hawklike features softened momentarily. 'Well, what about her?'

Cynthia Gilmore almost cringed under her husband's stern gaze. 'She's being very naughty, she –'

'Naughty? How in God's name can a 20-year-old woman be naughty? Talk sense, woman!'

The answer came in a rush. 'Not in her room, she wasn't in her room at breakfast time. You will eat alone in the mornings, you're so – so grumpy!'

'Not in her room. What are you saying, Cynthia? Rachel's vanished?'

'Yes! Yes!' The little woman wrung her hands in despair. 'I thought she'd gone riding but her horse is still in the livery.'

Brack Bowman's eyes were slits of dark fire in his handsome face.

'Judge! That envelope – the writin' looks mighty familiar. Open it, quick!'

The old man's hands trembled, then he pulled himself together with an effort. His shoulders sagged as he read aloud. 'By the time you get this we'll have your daughter in safe keeping. You have two weeks to raise $50,000: make the most of it. We will tell you where to bring the money. Come alone. Our eyes and ears are everywhere, so tell no one at all … NO ONE, or you will get her back in pieces small enough to make a pie. Remember, $50,000 and no talking!'

His grey eyes were pinpoints in a parchment face as he looked up at Brack.

'Tell me this is a joke, Mister Bowman.'

'It's no joke, judge. An' that's JJ's writin'. Just compare the letter to his statement. An' to think we assumed it was a kid, me, Wes, even JJ!'

Cynthia Gilmore was leaning heavily on the desk. Shock had robbed her of speech and turned her ruddy cheeks the colour of old putty. Considerably younger than her husband, she had suddenly aged to a point where she looked at least as old as him.

Brack spoke quietly. 'It'll be all right, folks. I got Carl Snell tied up real good. They won't have harmed your girl yet. An' Snell will sure as hell, beggin' yore pardon ma'am, tell me where to find her.'

Judge Gilmore opened the desk drawer and took out a painting about eight inches square. 'That's Rachel, our daughter. She's all we've got, Mister Bowman.'

Brack was goggling, eyes starting from his head.

Cynthia Gilmore was watching him, at last she forced words to her lips. 'She's our daughter, we love her. But she's hardly *that* beautiful Mr, er –'

'Bowman, ma'am, Brack Bowman.'

His eyes were still on the portrait. Shaking his head, he turned away to hide his face.

'We'll get her back OK, ma'am, me an' my brother.'

His head was spinning and his heart felt near to breaking. Rachel Gilmore. Golden hair falling softly into a roll on her shoulders, eyes like emeralds shining through the gold of her long lashes ... the lips a shade too full for perfection ... Lorna Bowman alive in another woman's portrait. What trick of nature had produced two such stunning blondes? His heart ached for his lost love, and his voice was gruff and thick.

'I've only ever seen one woman like that ... an' I married her. An' Snell murdered her as sure as if'n he shot her.'

Cynthia's hand flew to her mouth. 'Mayor Snell? He –'

'No, Mrs Gilmore, I'm talkin' 'bout his cousin Carl. The judge here knows all about it, don't you, judge?'

'Yes, yes, I do. I believe everything you've told me, Bowman. But it alters nothing as far as Lorens is concerned. Justice is justice. I'm not in the Texas Rangers now, you know.'

Brack's face became a frozen mask of hate. 'An' a dead daughter is a dead daughter, judge! Without Wes an' me her life ain't worth a java bean ... think about that!'

As he stood up, Judge Gilmore tried to look dignified holding onto the desk.

'You'd blackmail us? Let our daughter die? Why, it would be like allowing your wife to die all over again! And I won't be blackmailed young man, the law is above everything, and –'

Cynthia Gilmore flung herself at her husband and beat at him in a frenzy.

'Above our daughter's life? You're not human. I don't know you any more. You're just Judge Gilmore, a thing, not a person!'

Brack spoke quietly. 'For your sake, ma'am, we'll get your daughter back. Fact is, I wouldn't sleep nights if'n I let her die. But you, Judge Gilmore, I hope you burn in hell ... an' I ain't finished with you yet!'

The judge's face mottled with anger, but before he could speak there was a tap at the door.

'That'll be Mayor Snell,' he got out hoarsely. 'Come!' he shouted, but his voice quavered.

Mayor Snell entered smiling uncertainly. He was a short, plump man with the air of a busy undertaker. Clad in a black suit, he kept wringing his hands and bobbing his bald head.

'Afternoon, judge an' you, ma'am,' he oiled. His eyes fell on Brack and he squinted at him short-sightedly. 'Do I know you, mister? I've seen –'

'Yeah, name's Bowman, remember? I've lost my beard.'

The mayor gulped nervously. 'Oh yes, unfortunate business that, very ... and your wife too – yes, er, very sad, but, er, water under the bridge, eh?'

'Not quite, mayor. Sit down. The judge has something to tell you.'

Judge Gilmore looked at the mayor, then at Brack. 'Should we tell him? Can we trust him?'

'Tell him everythin'. I reckon he'll help us convict his cousin ... that oughta help Wes. The rest you can leave to me.'

The mayor's eyes widened. 'Convict my cousin? Oh dear, what's he been up to now? I wish he'd stayed in England –'

Cynthia Gilmore sat close to her husband as he unfolded the full story to the astonished and horrified mayor. He dealt with the two statements and Carl Snell's notebook and summed up as succinctly as for a jury.

Brack added a rider. 'If'n you say one word outside this room I'll hunt you down an' throw your head in a rattler's pit an' that's a promise!'

Mayor Snell darted a glance at him and shivered. 'Er, yes, I'm sure you would: How can I help?'

'Write a statement of all you know about your cousin. Not hearsay, just facts. Do it now,' Judge Gilmore said heavily, as he handed him a pen and several sheets of paper.

The mayor smiled sickly. 'Judge, you aren't exactly breaking my heart ... just so long as he can't get at me after.'

The judge regarded him coldly. 'In this country kidnapping carries the death penalty, and kidnapping my daughter won't help him one bit!'

Brack laughed mirthlessly. 'An' if'n you don't

hang him, judge, I sure as hell will. So he won't trouble you, mayor, less'n he bothers you as a ghost.'

Cynthia Gilmore was dabbing her eyes with a lace handkerchief.

'You've got him in your custody, Mr Bowman. How can you rescue my daughter? It would appear that those who abducted her don't know Mr Lorens abducted Snell at almost the same time. Where will they have taken her?'

Brack smiled again like Satan counting souls. 'When I've held a live rattler next to his face he'll tell me anythin' I need. Well, he'll write it down. Fact is, he ain't talkin' too well since Wes's foot got friendly with his jaw!'

Mayor Snell interrupted squeakily, 'It's almost certain your daughter is being held at the ranch. Carl's got an attic room he's been doing up real swell. He's English, as you know.'

Brack said quietly as he headed for the door, 'Well, I got a way of findin' out, I got a way of gettin' in. Ain't no reason you should fret at all, Mrs Gilmore.'

He stared stonily at the judge. 'Don't get tempted to raise an army to storm the ranch. It only takes a millionth of a second for a bullet to blow your girl's head off.'

'They wouldn't would they?' Cynthia whispered.

'Why not, ma'am? Kidnappin' means hangin'. Can't hang a man twice, can you?'

Judge Gilmore seemed to have shrunk.

'We're relying on you and Lorens. Come back

with her, please. And about Lorens, we, er, might be able to arrange a light sentence. But a pardon is out of the question.'

Brack stabbed a powerful finger at him. 'We'll be back. You an' I ain't finished yet, judge, not by a long ways.'

TWENTY

To Brack Bowman the ride back to the soddy shack seemed never-ending. Tired and angry, he would have taken shelter to snooze had it not been for visions of the lovely Rachel in the hands of a hired killer. God only knew what the man might be doing to her whilst vainly awaiting Carl Snell's return. His fear and anger kept his features hard and bleak despite the thought of the frantic search the ranch gunnies must have conducted through the night. It must have seemed to them that the ground had opened up and swallowed Snell, as if he had never existed.

At length Brack pulled up his horse and took a swig at his canteen. Stunted cacti blurred and danced through a heat haze as he narrowed his eyes against the eye-blasting glitter of gypsum. The reflection of rock and gypsum beneath the incandescent furnace of the afternoon sun seemed to burn deep into his skull. He removed his Plainsman hat and mopped sweat from his brow. When he poured the last of his water into the hat, his horse drank greedily. Once the animal had finished he set off at a hard gallop towards the low range of hills.

It was late afternoon when he slid from his saddle and hurried into the soddy. Quickly he told Wes all that had happened.

'Well, brother,' Wes grinned, 'we seem to have ole Snell well cooked!'

Carl Snell's face was badly swollen and he still spat blood from time to time. His thoughts spun giddily as he listened to the brothers' conversation. What hope could there be for him now? If he couldn't escape....

Brack turned to him. 'Is she in the attic room? Would your gunnie have taken her there during the night?'

Snell spat at him and closed his eyes.

JJ spoke up in a hoarse whisper. 'Mister Snell, ain't no use givin' these fellers a chance to make you talk. Believe me they'll make you talk an' they'll enjoy doin' it.'

Snell's eyes were venomous. 'Go to hell,' he groaned.

Brack eased alongside him and took the swollen blue-black jaws in his hands. 'Is she in the attic, Snell?' he asked quietly.

The injured man's eyes bugged wide with pain as the vice-like grip pressed relentlessly harder on his broken jaw.

'Shit Brack!' Wes burst out. 'You're actin' like a monster, do —'

Brack yelled over his shoulder at him, 'That girl is alone with this bastard's men! God knows what they'll be doin' … you think I should treat him gentle? I'm goin' to poke his eyes out in two minutes, after I'm through pulpin' his jaw.'

He released his grip momentarily. 'Is she in the attic, do you think?'

Snell nodded weakly. 'Yegh,' he gurgled before he fainted.

Wes smiled tightly. 'You sure got a way with you, brother!'

Brack went to one of his bags and hunted through it.

'You sure you ain't got a piano in there?' Wes enquired.

Brack held up an old-fashioned crossbow and some wicked steel-tipped short arrows.

'Bowman by name, bowman by nature!' he grunted as he slung the crossbow over his broad shoulders and shoved the arrows into a little cloth drawstring bag. He checked his Peacemaker and buckled a fresh cartridge belt around his waist.

'Where are you goin'?' Wes asked. 'If'n you're goin' down that hole I reckon I oughta go along, brother.'

'You stay here Wes,' Brack ordered. 'Look after these jaspers.'

His face brooked no argument and Wes nodded assent.

'OK, look out for yourself, Brack. I don't want to lose my brother now I've just found him … an' you ain't got me to save your skin this time!'

Brack made his way through the tunnel as

quickly as he dared, and was soon at the bottom of
the well. He paused only long enough to wipe the
sweat from his eyes, then climbed to the top to
peer cautiously over the edge.

A thin, heavily bearded gnome of a man leaned
against the wall of the ranch house next to the
door. His attention was fixed on the quirly he was
rolling and his carbine was propped on the
veranda rails. Brack's eyes were drawn by a face
at the attic window. A beautiful, tear-streaked
face framed by long, fair hair, and a blue
high-collared dress. In the dim lamplight of the
room he saw the dark figure of a man, and then
the thick-fingered hand which grabbed her
shoulder and wrenched her away from the
window.

Brack slipped an arrow into his crossbow and
squinted along it at the bearded gnome who drew
on his quirly and exhaled luxuriously. Blue smoke
trickled from his nostrils and mouth and drifted
skywards. He cocked his head as he heard the
swoosh of the arrow which hammered through his
neck and pinned him to the wall where he stood.
He was dead before he had a clue what was
happening.

A second man appeared from behind the ranch
and joined the gnome. 'All quiet Walt,' he said as
he sat down on the veranda steps. He glanced up
at Walt in amazement. 'You ain't sleepin' again
Walt? If Snell comes back an' –'

Brack's second arrow caught him dead-centre
below the breastbone and a thin red trickle ran

from each corner of his mouth to drip into his lap. He stood and crumpled forward.

Brack dropped the crossbow and hurried to the door, pausing only to prop the body up against the steps alongside the impaled Walt. Once inside he spied an open-plan staircase and went up two at a time, his Colt Peacemaker gripped in his fist.

At the top of the stairs he came to a little gallery, and through an open door he glimpsed a short, narrow staircase.

The huge hand clamped on that blue-clad shoulder was engraved in fire on his brain. With two bounds he was at the attic door.

Every sinew twitching with suppressed fury, he listened alertly. The man was speaking in a deep bass, slowly but thickly as if he'd been hitting the whiskey.

'Snell ain't here, sweetheart. Gawd knows if'n he'll come back, 'cos his rannies ain't got no idea where or when he went ... an' he owed me $200 for deliverin' you safe 'n sound.' He paused and belched loudly. 'Pardon *me*, Miss Goldilocks,' he went on with heavy sarcasm. 'My manners ain't good 'nuff, is that it? Waal, Miss High 'n Mighty Judge's Daughter, I reckon, seein' as I ain't been paid, I own you till I collect, and –' he belched again, 'we might as well just carry on here havin' a little fun until old Snell gits back ... if'n he ever does.'

In the silence Brack heard a soft whimper and the sound of a belt buckle unclipping.

'Waasa matter, girlie?' slurred the ruffian. 'Ain't

this big 'nuff for you?'

Brack waited no longer. The door splintered to matchwood as he hurtled into the room.

A huge man the size of a grizzly bear was advancing on a cowering, blonde-haired girl. Brack registered every detail of the scene with lightning-flare vividness. Her dress torn off, clad in a white camisole which hugged her slim body tightly and hid none of her charms, Rachel Gilmore was even lovelier than her portrait. Her green eyes were wide with terror and a small fist was pressed to soft lips as the villain towered over her. At the sight of her, Brack's heart missed a beat. His breath rasping, Grizzly seemed unaware of the shattered door and the peril behind him.

Brack hissed in a voice that wasn't his own, 'Leave that girl alone, mister! I want you!'

Grizzly turned with the deceptive speed that big men often have. 'You take your turn, feller! You kin have a go when I've shook the starch outa her ass.'

Not wanting to bring the whole gang running, Brack leathered his Peacemaker.

'I'm goin' to kill you with my bare hands,' he grated, as he advanced on the huge man.

A ponderous right-hander would have taken off his head if he hadn't moved. He stepped lazily outside the punch and followed up with his elbow to the man's gut. It was not at all flabby, and Brack realized that this was a man of colossal strength: whatever happened he had to keep out of reach of those enormous arms. A brain-scrambling left landed high over Brack's ear and hurled him into the corner next to the girl. Desperately they both rolled away as the huge man jumped in with both feet in an attempt to crush Brack's chest.

Springing up, Brack kicked out fiercely and saw teeth shoot from his opponent's mouth. The villain spat blood and grinned dangerously as he rose to his feet.

'Amusin' little fucker, ain't you?' he grunted and reached for Brack with outspread arms.

Brack grabbed two of the banana-like fingers and jerked them apart; at the same time he kicked the man in the crotch. He felt testicles shatter under the force of his kick and the big man bent double in agony. His face sank nicely to meet Brack's knee and he straightened up to walk into a thunderous right-hander. As he tottered backwards, Brack moved in to finish off the fight. Then disaster struck as Brack's foot slipped on a small rug and he fell on his back. His head thunked on the pine floor and stars pin-wheeled into darkness.

He could only have lost consciousness for a moment. As his vision cleared he saw the axe. Somehow the big man had snatched it from the wall and was poised on the balls of his feet over Brack, on the point of striking.

Rachel Gilmore moved like lightning. Seizing the man's gun from the table where he had laid it, she shrieked, 'Stop!'

The wrecked face turned slowly towards her. Blood sprayed her chest and camisole as he spat disgustedly.

'You ain't got the guts, lady!'

He leaned back and raised the axe higher.

With a crash like a clap of thunder in the confined room the gun went off. Brack's nose wrinkled at the smell of cordite as the far side of the gunnie's head mushroomed outwards. Then the whole head ballooned to engulf the mushroom and exploded. Shards of bone, brains and teeth were broadcast in sheets of blood all over the whitewashed walls and pine floor.

'That's done it,' he muttered as he grabbed Rachel by a bare arm that was as cold as marble, and pulled her through the door. 'The whole damn gang of 'em will be down on our necks.'

In a daze the girl allowed herself to be tugged along behind her tall, lean rescuer. He was speaking again, but what was he saying? The ringing in her ears from the gunshot had all but blotted out her hearing.

'Climb down inside the well. If'n I don't make it you gotta follow the tunnel all the way to the end, then climb up an' holler for help. Got it? Got it?' he shouted. His words seemed to be muffled as if he spoke through a thick blanket but she got the gist of it.

From the veranda they saw men hurrying towards them, guns at the ready. A slug splintered the door behind them.

Someone was shouting, 'Who's that feller? Don't shoot the girl! Get that bastard with her! What in hell's wrong with Walt an' Harry?'

Brack gave Rachel a shove and she sprinted for

the well, her camisole a white blur in the darkness. In a few moments she gained it and climbed over the rim. Arriving close behind, he crouched alongside her and the nearness of her shoulder and arm, the subtle scent she used, made his head swim.

'Go on down,' he grunted. 'Hang on tight to the handholds. I'll be right behind you soon as I can.'

She looked down and saw that she still gripped the big man's gun in a bloodstained hand.

'I'll stay with you, I can fire –'

Brack shook his head angrily as a slug ricocheted from the sloping roof of the well with a vicious whine.

'Dammit, will you do as you're told? Get down that well! Now! An' leave that gun.'

Her eyes travelled over him swiftly; she liked what she saw.

'OK, boss,' she chuckled, and was gone.

With a sigh of relief that at last she was safe, he sprinted back to the veranda, dodging the spurts of dust from a fusillade of gunfire. The gnome-like man was still pinned to the wall and Brack grabbed his carbine. His companion sat bolt upright beside him and Brack snatched his pistol too, before rolling over and emptying the carbine into two gunnies a mere ten yards away. Three more were crouching down, taking careful aim at him. He shot one through the head with his pistol and another dropped his gun and howled in pain. The third one slammed a bullet into the veranda only inches away, and Brack emptied the pistol in his direction before dashing for the well. The big man's gun was on the rim where Rachel had left it; he used it to good effect and saw the third man keel over as a slug took him between the eyes.

A head popped round the corner of the bunkhouse. 'Hey mister, hold on. Who the hell are you?'

'A ratcatcher!' Brack yelled as he drew his Peacemaker.

The man called out again, a note of fear shredding his voice, 'Listen friend, you killed Red an' Butch, an' Tom … an' probably that jasper we ain't seen afore. What's it all about? We'd like to know afore we rub you out!'

Another voice from behind one of the outhouses joined in. 'You got anythin' to do with Mr Snell's disappearance?'

'Yeah! We kidnapped him, just the way he snatched the lady,' Brack called. 'You fellers ain't got no chance 'cos he'll name you all.'

'Kidnappin'!' the first man howled. 'What in hell have we got to do with kidnappin'!?'

By way of reply Brack took aim and squeezed off a couple of shots at a face peering through the bunkhouse window. There was a scream of agony as slivers of glass ripped into the pale features.

'I asked 'bout kidnappin' mister. We don't know nuthin' 'bout no kidnappin',' the first man shouted again.

'You mean you didn't see the lady ride in with that goddam great grizzly bear in the night?'

'Yeah, I seen her, but I thought they was just visitin', I ain't never seen either of 'em afore.'

As he sat up, Brack kept his eyes peeled.

'You'll wish you never saw her, you bastards. She's Judge Gilmore's daughter! An' in case you don't know it, he used to be a Texas Ranger, so there ain't nowhere you kin hide from his buddies if'n I don't kill you!'

His listener digested this information with a cold hand of fear squeezing at his heart. He knew that the Rangers weren't bound by the Army code, they'd cross the border into Mexico to snatch a man if they wanted him badly enough. There was nowhere to hide.

'Lissen friend,' he called. 'We don't know nuthin' about Miss Gilmore, 'cept she came in the night an' you jest pushed her down that well. If'n you broke her neck it ain't nuthin' to do with us!'

Brack spotted a movement behind the shattered window and put a slug into the frame. From the corner of his eye he saw another movement to his right behind a water-butt, and he rolled over to aim. At the same instant two men with Winchesters opened up from the bunkhouse window.

Pain whiplashed white fire across his forehead and blood stung in his eyes. Instinctively he loosed off two shots. No sense in letting them see he was hurt …

'Hold your fire, fellers,' shouted the man behind the outhouse. 'We gotta think this out. If'n the judge knows Snell took his daughter, the whole world will fall on us, like as not.'

'That's right, Pete,' yelled another. 'I only come here 'cos the pay was good, I jest guard the damn place, I ain't aimin' to be in a necktie party 'cos Snell is fool enough to kidnap a bloody judge's daughter....'

In the cool night breeze that had sprung up, Brack's wound stopped bleeding as the blood congealed. His head was light and swimming and, as he shook it to clear his dizziness, cold sweat stuck his shirt to his back. 'Now or never,' he thought, alarmed by his weakness, and swung himself over the edge of the well. He climbed down a few steps until his eyes were level with the rim.

'He's in that damn well,' a hoarse voice exulted. 'He ain't gonna git far now!'

Brack grinned tautly and squeezed off a shot at a leg just visible from behind the water-butt. The owner screamed repeatedly as the heavy slug shattered his knee before travelling up his thigh to lodge in his pelvis. Taking advantage of the distraction of the yells echoing round the ranch, Brack descended to the bottom of the well, grabbed his crossbow from where he'd left it and wriggled through into the mine shaft. Replacing the rock, he fumbled for the oil lamp. As he lit it he heard a sob of relief. Rachel was there, her arms folded tightly on her breasts, huddled in the dark like a lost child.

Silently, he cursed himself for forgetting to tell her about the oil lamp. Her glorious hair was matted round her shoulders which were rashed with gooseflesh and her eyes were bright with unshed tears. Alone in the cold, dark well, she must have feared that each gunshot, each scream of agony meant his death, have lived out in hideous detail the vision of being recaptured. In the smoky yellow light it seemed that Lorna was alive once more, haunted, terrified half out of her wits. With iron self-control he held himself back from speaking his wife's name, as he put a comforting arm around her.

At once she turned to him, her slim arms clutching him like a vice as she buried her face in his chest and wept. Her wracking sobs tore at his heart and suddenly he found his lips brushing the tears from her smudged cheeks.

'Did you see his head? Oh God, his head, his head!' she moaned piteously. Brack placed the lamp on a ledge and held her tightly.

'Miss,' he breathed in her ear. 'If'n you hadn't lost your head an' shot him, I'd have lost mine for sure. That axe of his'n was sure dyin' to kiss my neck.'

As he held onto her and stroked her hair the sobs which shuddered through her slender body stirred Brack irresistibly. At length she cried herself out and tilted up her face. Before he could stop himself his lips were on hers fiercely, possessively. Years of loneliness and misery melted away and he fought to stem a rising tide of passion.

Somehow he managed to pull away and a blush of embarrassment burned his cheeks.

She smiled up at him shakily. 'And I don't even know your name!'

'Brack, Brack Bowman, miss, an' –'

'Brack? I like it, you must call me Rachel. My father is –'

'Yeah, I know, we've met,' he replied wearily as he released her and leaned against the tunnel wall. Dizziness blurred his vision and his head throbbed sickeningly.

Her eyes widened at the blood drying on his face. 'Oh, Brack, you're hurt!' she cried. 'We've got to get you to a doctor!'

With the tunnel reeling around him, he steadied himself and took up the lamp. 'OK, Rachel, let's go, watch out for potholes.'

She slipped a bare arm round his waist, 'And you mind your head, you've taken enough knocks already,' she warned, her coldness and fears forgotten in concern for this handsome, rawboned man who had rescued her from a nightmare.

Admiringly, Wes watched the beautiful girl, dressed in a spare pair of Levis and plaid shirt from Brack's bag, as she worked on his brother's wound. Gently she'd sponged the dried blood from his cheeks with a bandanna and was bandaging the red furrow in his brow with another.

'This is gettin' a mite ridiculous, Brack. There's these two jaspers, Miss Rachel, you'n me … an' only two durned hosses between the two o' us!'

Rachel spoke over her shoulder. 'May I make a suggestion, please?'

'Sure, miss, I'd appreciate it.'

'Well, Brack's concussed and likely to fall off a horse. Both he and Mr Snell need medical attention. So why don't you ride into Lewis and return with a buckboard big enough for six?'

Wes's brow wrinkled with uncertainty. 'Good thinkin', but why six?'

'To save you riding back here and then back to Lewis. Three trips would be exhausting. You could use a driver,' she finished in a matter of fact tone.

Wes was still frowning, then he chuckled. 'You sure got a good brain on you, Miss Rachel. But I can't leave you here, so you can ride with me an' –'

She tossed her head impatiently. 'What, and leave Brack here on his own with these gentlemen? Suppose he was taken ill? He's lost a lot of blood, you know.'

Brack grunted as he drank hot tea laced with whiskey. 'You get home to your folks soon's you can, Rachel. They're mighty worried. I'll be OK, an' what're they goin' to think if'n you're alone with me 'cept for these –'

'I'm staying with you, Brack.' Her voice was warm but authoritative, faintly tinged with a hint of mischief. 'And it's dark now, I'm afraid of riding in the dark with strange men.'

Wes rolled his eyes. 'Well, there you are, Brack. Guess we got our orders!' He smiled gravely at the blonde-haired girl, 'I'll call on your folks. Take care of my brother while I'm gone … he needs a lotta lookin' after! He's always getting near killed.'

'Ha ha,' Brack growled. 'Here, take this damn

letter with you or we might never see you again; an' remember, it's my reputation you might sully!'

At first, thinking he was alluding to being alone with her except for the two securely bound prisoners while his brother was away, Rachel smiled shyly. Then she sobered as Brack handed over the letter. 'What's that letter? Why –'

'It's a long story, Rachel. I'll tell you later,' Brack interrupted and stretched wearily. 'Go on, Mister Lorens, on your way,' he joked as Wes stood peering doubtfully into the darkness.

'Yes sir, Mister Bowman, sir!' Wes replied with a laugh and ducked out of the door of the soddy.

Rachel was shaking her head with a puzzled frown. 'If he's your brother ... why is he called Lorens? You're –'

'That's all part of the long story, Rachel.'

'Well,' she smiled, her green eyes shining in a way that set his heart racing, 'time is something we've plenty of. So, how about telling me?'

Brack nodded assent. Snell had sunk into a coma-like sleep, his blue-black jaws hanging open, and the one-eared Jake James had also dozed off. It was as good a time as any he'd ever have. As his story unfolded Rachel listened with fascination.

At last he concluded, 'An' you know the rest, after I got into the ranch....'

She looked away, a lump in her throat. Two spots of red burned high on her cheeks and her lovely eyes flashed.

'You risked your life to save me, even after father refused to pardon your brother?'

Brack smiled wryly. 'It wasn't my intention to force the judge. I wasn't makin' it a condition or nothin'. What kinda man would leave you in the hands of vermin like Snell?'

'You think he wouldn't have released me if my father had paid the ransom?' she asked, biting her lip.

He weighed his words carefully, 'Well, Rachel, I reckon he had plans for you. Snell's cousin said the attic room was all done up recent. A critter like that couldn't afford to let you go, not after he'd had his fun with you. No, you were dead from the moment that big feller abducted you.'

She shuddered and her hand sought his. 'Thank you, Brack ... I'll, er, make it up to you, that's a promise.'

The lean, rangy man blushed to the roots of his hair, even the tips of his ears reddened as he took refuge in reloading his Peacemaker. It was no use trying to pretend that he wasn't mighty taken with her. Whenever he looked at her his heart thudded madly and memories of their embrace in the mineshaft shimmered in his mind. The timbre of her voice, the way she moved, the gleam of lamplight in her blonde hair, all made him yearn to take her in his arms and smother her with kisses ... to say nothing of her uncanny resemblance to his lost wife....

'I'm sore in need of a wash an' change of clothes, Rachel. If'n you could just step outside a while I'd appreciate it,' he said.

'And I need some air, it's very smoky in here,

isn't it?' she laughed.

As soon as she was gone, he washed and changed into a pair of black corduroys, black shirt and scarf. Then he pulled on black, elaborately tooled soft leather boots and a pair of silver Mexican spurs. Lastly he buckled on a new cartridge belt and tied the holster of his Peacemaker onto his thigh with a length of black rawhide. As he stowed his discarded clothing and the crossbow in his bag he couldn't help grinning.

'No wonder ole Wes thought I'd got a piano in there,' he thought. 'His face was sure a picture when I took that crossbow out!' He recalled the day when he bought the bow in a little town called Arkwright ... a peaceful town with a tough sheriff. He had only stayed one night before riding on to a town on the Mexican border, looking for Wes!

With that bow he'd silently disposed of three gunnies round a log cabin, then he'd gone in and shot it out with a killer who had terrorized all the towns in fifty square miles. And now ... not bad for a five-dollar crossbow!

Wes returned late the following afternoon. He'd hired a buckboard, and had possessed the foresight to bring fresh steak and bread for a good meal before the return to Lewis.

'I see you've had a shave. Don't suppose you brought a razor, Wes?' Brack enquired, fingering his stubble.

Like a travelling magician his brother whipped a razor from the pocket of his jerkin. 'Can't have you goin' to see the judge lookin' like a filthy trail yahoo.' His eyes ran over Brack's change of clothing. 'Ain't it time you changed them ole duds?' he asked innocently. 'Miss Gilmore will be ashamed of bein' seen with a roughneck like you!'

Rachel's laugh was low and musical. 'Daddy will just love that! To think his only daughter spent the night with the brother of a wanted man!'

Then her eyes grew sombre as she walked over to Wes and gazed into his face. 'Wes Lorens … when I've finished with my father he'll likely give you a medal of honour! Take my word for it, he'll pardon you.'

She turned to Brack, her eyes aglow. 'And what will he make of a wanted man like you, I wonder?'

'I ain't wanted, Rachel, not since –'

'Oh yes you are, Brack Bowman,' she murmured. 'I want you, and I'm thoroughly spoilt … I always get what I want!'

Brack felt his heart pound erratically. 'Well, Rachel, I'll sure do my best to see you keep on gettin' spoilt,' he answered. 'Now how 'bout cookin' those steaks so's we can hit the trail before dark?'

It was just after nightfall when the buckboard drew up outside the Blue Star. Snell and James lay tied securely on the wooden bed of the rig. As soon as they saw her, Judge Gilmore and his wife leapt to their feet to embrace their daughter. Wes and Brack stood to one side and smiled to see the reunion.

'Daddy, the smoke in here!' Rachel choked, pulling free of the judge's arms. 'How many –'

'Ten cigars in the last three hours,' Cynthia Gilmore told her. 'You've no idea how many more in the last two days!'

The old man held Rachel at arm's length and inspected her critically. 'Are you hurt? What did those devils do to you?' he demanded.

'I'm fine, daddy, thanks to Brack and his brother.'

The judge eyed the twin brothers appraisingly.

'Ah, Bowman, you're the one with the grey sideburns. I noticed the difference when Lorens visited me this morning with the good news.'

'Well, judge,' Brack drawled, 'he's the one who needs the pardon.'

The old man's lips tightened. 'You've saved me $50,000 dollars, gentlemen, but I –'

Rachel faced him angrily. 'But nothing! They saved you $50,000 and my life! Those men had no intention of letting me go after … after....'

In a voice that shook with a mixture of annoyance at his daughter's defiance and fear and relief at her return, the judge demanded imperiously, 'Where is Snell now? Do you have –'

'Tied up nice an' secure out in the buckboard, judge; him an' Jake James, the guy who wrote the kidnap demand. I told you 'bout him,' Wes replied.

'Yes and I've been studying those documents you left, and –'

Wes interrupted, stabbing a finger at Carl Snell's notebook on the table. 'There's enough evidence in that to hang him ten times over. An' a statement he was obligin' enough to sign, seein' he ain't talkin' so well.'

With a chill smile the judge held out his hand. 'I want to say thank you, gentlemen. My wife and I are both truly grateful, but I think that $2,000 should –'

Brack stepped across the room. He loomed above the judge, his fist clenched with fury, and gritted, 'Wes an' I don't want a cent for rescuin' a girl from hellhounds! What sort of men do you take us for? An' I got a small fortune my ma left me. We don't even want your thanks. But I want you to think real hard about my brother's pardon. An' another thing, I ain't forgettin' you took four years outa my life for nuthin'.'

Judge Gilmore stared back at him, and took a deep breath. 'Suit yourselves about the money. I must say I respect your integrity. But the law is the law. It is above all of us. I can't go handing out reprieves and pardons like, like ... well, I just can't compromise my judicial function.'

'Judge,' Brack told him grimly, 'you just read them things again. We gotta visit the doc afore Snell dies ... I ain't about to let him cheat the hangman. We'll be back in the mornin'. If'n you can't see your way to clear Wes you might just be sorry.'

Judge Gilmore's cheeks burned with twin spots of colour. His hands gripped the edge of his desk until the knuckles whitened.

'How dare you threaten me. A circuit judge?

You know the –'

Rachel stood beside Brack. Her eyes shone as she took his hand.

'Daddy, I love this man. There's no need to look so shocked. It doesn't take a lifetime to discover about love.'

Her father's mouth opened to frame a sharp retort but, before he could speak, she told him about the abduction, her near-rape at the hands of the bear-like gunman, how Brack had come near to death to save her, and how she'd had to kill the big man....

'I spent last night in his arms, and I want to marry him ... if he'll have me. After all, daddy,' she finished with a defiant tilt to her chin, 'I'm a killer!'

Brack laughed, his lean features lighting up with joy. 'If'n I'll have you? Rachel, if you don't marry me I'm gonna kidnap you myself!'

Judge Gilmore wasn't known as 'Old Granite' for nothing. 'Marriage? We'll see about that, and it doesn't alter –'

'Doesn't alter your decision, Judge Gilmore?' Cynthia intervened with deceptive mildness. 'Now, I have something to say. If you don't arrange a pardon for Wesley, I shall call you Judge Gilmore and treat you that way forever. Do you want to play with your grandson some day?' she enquired, still in the same gentle tone. 'Do you? Listen, you stubborn old man, if you go on behaving like a legal martinet, we'll never see Rachel again.'

Before he could answer Rachel added her voice to that of her mother. 'Daddy, please yourself whether you listen to mum. But I'll tell you this, she's absolutely right. If you don't do what Brack asks I'll go with him right now. You'll never see me, or any grandchildren, ever!'

Judge Gilmore felt his age all at once. Slumping into the chair behind his desk, he picked up the notebook. For twenty minutes the room was silent except for the occasional rustle of paper as he turned the pages.

Finally, he pushed the book away and rubbed his eyes. 'I should have considered the weight of evidence more carefully before giving judgment,' he said with a rueful smile. 'When's the wedding?'

Brack grinned back at him. 'Just as soon's I've tied up the last loose end.'

'Loose end? You mean as soon as Wes gets legal possession of the ranch?' Rachel asked quickly.

'No, Wes'll see to that OK. There's one thing I got to do.'

Her heart missed a beat as she saw the steely glint of his eyes. 'What is it, Brack?' she murmured.

'There's a Mister Frankie Dorrell who shot our pa in the back still on the loose. I want him dancin' alongside Snell. I'm goin' to bring him in.'

Seeing the pallor of Rachel's face, Wes drawled easily, 'Maybe he's one of the varmints you killed on the ranch. You seem to have gotten most on 'em!'

'No, Wes, JJ told me Dorrell left a month ago.'

Rachel gripped his arm and gazed at him imploringly. 'Please, Brack! Don't go away, not now!'

'Go? Who said anythin' about goin' any place?'

'But you said –'

He kissed her hair. 'I'm sorry, darlin'. Dorrell ain't more'n fifty yards off. He's the new owner of the Yellow Dog. Fittin' name for a back-shootin' rattler like him, ain't it?'

He turned to the judge and smiled broadly. 'Gonna be back real soon. Then I reckon it'll be time to celebrate. Any chance of a cigar an' a cup of coffee?'